ℰMMA
in love

Emma Tennant is the author of many distinguished novels, including *The Bad Sister*, *Wild Nights*, *Two Women of London* and *Faustine* (reprinted as *Travesties* in 1995). With *Pemberley* (1993), *An Unequal Marriage* (1994) and *Elinor and Marianne* (1996) she has created a new literary genre, now much emulated, the classic progression.

EMMA *in love*

JANE AUSTEN'S *EMMA* CONTINUED

EMMA TENNANT

FOURTH ESTATE • *London*

To Sabine

EMMA
in love

Part One

1

*E*mma Knightley, handsome, married and rich, with a comfortable home and a doating husband, seemed to unite some of the best blessings of existence, and had lived nearly four years since her marriage with very little to distress or vex her.

She had suffered, it was true, at the death of her father Mr. Woodhouse, a loss brought about by the catching of a cold at Hartfield, where Emma and Mr. Knightley attended to his every need; and she had suffered again when her sister Isabella, seven years her senior, had died shortly after, in London, of a fever. But the gratitude felt at the order in which parent and sibling had succumbed to mortality soon supplanted the real grief Emma felt at that time; for Mr. Woodhouse could not criticise

Isabella's doctor for his negligence, having departed this world himself; and Isabella, already ill on the first occasion of her father's sitting unwontedly in a draught, had neither desire nor capacity to give vent to her mistrust of Mr. Perry.

Two years had Emma lived at the centre of Mr. Knightley's estate, Donwell Abbey; and for all the suggestions put forward by those in Highbury who considered it advisable to give opinions on the renovations required by an ancient house, neither she nor Mr. Knightley had so much as touched a stone or added a wing. Despite the pleas of Mrs. Elton and her friends, visitors to the Vicarage and thus, by sheer force of convention, occasional guests at Donwell Abbey, Mr. and Mrs. Knightley declared themselves content with the place as old Mr. Knightley had left it. There was no need for a prospect.— It was pleasant enough to pass down the lime walk and discover from there the pretty stream that made a boundary with the Abbey Mill Farm; if one were fortunate, the sight of apple blossom or gently rising smoke might be augmented by a glimpse of Mrs. Martin, who lived as happily at the farmhouse with her husband as Mr. and Mrs. Knightley were seen to do at the main house. Emma was satisfied, or so it was judged, with all she had been given in life; and at twenty-five years of age might earnestly look forward to many years in surroundings that were in no need whatsoever of modernisation or improvement.

The real evils of Emma's situation lay in the power of having had too much her own way since she was a child. It was considered by those who were her friends (of whom Mrs. Weston was the most devoted) that Emma's resistance to change at Donwell Abbey reflected her inclination to remain a loved daughter all her days rather than a wife.

There was also a disposition, as Mrs. Weston was aware, in the young mistress of Donwell Abbey to think a little too well of herself; she had been loved excessively by her father, who could find no fault in her; and Mr. Knightley, who once had lectured and blamed Emma if ever he felt it to be necessary, was now careful to hold himself in check, should an occasion arise that would in the past have provoked a rebuff. Emma was, in short, marooned on an island of self-regard, where any idea of a different outlook was instantly turned away. It was not only the old house, which seemed to belong to another age altogether, which its mistress wished to keep just as it was. Mrs. Weston feared for Emma herself.— But Mrs. Weston, in the days she had been "poor Miss Taylor" to Emma's father, had been a governess; and, for all the very real amicability that existed between herself and the châtelaine of Donwell Abbey, there was nonetheless a marked reluctance on the part of Emma to listen to her advice.

"Dear Emma!" said Mrs. Weston, on the occasion of her coming for a strawberry-picking at the Abbey, "I do wish you would go away with Mr. Knightley somewhere.— Why, he has talked of it himself, and says you do not give him an answer. When you returned here, you know, you would see that the rooms you sit in – even if only those – could be made over very prettily.— I saw some new papers myself, sent down to me by Mr. Weston's son Frank—"

Here Mrs. Weston stopped, and bit her lip. Highbury, though it had grown more populous in the years since Emma's marriage to Mr. Knightley, and there were many newcomers unacquainted with the past history of the principal landowner and the other residents, still speculated on whether there should have been a match between Miss Woodhouse and Mr. Weston's son Frank Churchill. The very idea had seemed perfect; and Emma had surely been in favour of it before her attention had been drawn to the neighbour who had all her life cared for her and lavished attentions on her father; this being Mr. Knightley. Besides this, there was the small matter of Mr. Churchill's announcing he was in love with Jane Fairfax – but Highbury thought little of that unfortunate young woman now, since her abandonment almost at the church door and Frank's disappearance to Yorkshire. Here, he was said to have married an heiress specified in his aunt's will. But the village grew irascible that so few details were known of the marriage, and Mrs. Weston was duly punished for her refusal to divulge them.

It was no wonder that the mention of her stepson's name, unintentional though it appeared to be, should cause Mrs. Weston to cease her strawberry-picking and suggest, with the familiarity to which she was happily accustomed on her visits to Donwell Abbey, that a glass of lemon water would not come amiss.

"I have no need to travel abroad," replied Emma – for she knew her friend well enough to realise a change of subject was hastily sought, and out of mischief she would not supply it. "And I do not desire new papers on the walls of my rooms, dear Mrs. Weston. Everything is perfect as it stands. I am surprised you do not concur – why, you are come to resemble Mrs. Elton at the Vicarage, with her birds of paradise and her talk of patriotic wallpapers brought in from France. I thought you liked to come here and find all unchanged; after the sad decline in gentility of the village and its new denizens, I would have thought you grateful to be here!"

"No, no, Emma, you misunderstand me!" cried Mrs. Weston, who was disturbed at the sudden loss of composure in her friend. "There is no place more lovely than the Abbey. I am of that opinion and I shall never change it. But Frank's letter – his news—"

Here Mr. Knightley, seeking his wife in the Abbey

gardens, strolled down towards the strawberry beds, remarking as he came that he had hardly expected to find the ladies so hard at work in the heat of the day.

"Come in, Emma! And you, Mrs. Weston – why, you are in need of refreshment, that is as clear to me as the nose on my face. My beloved, have you not offered Mrs. Weston a glass of lemon water? My brother will be happy to join you, Mrs. Weston, if Emma forgets."

Emma looked away in annoyance, but followed Mr. Knightley and Mrs. Weston into the stone parlour of the house, where refreshment was duly brought. She could not refrain from wishing that Mr. Knightley had not come to search for her at that moment; she had wanted to speak to Mrs. Weston of his brother John Knightley, who was recently arrived at the Abbey with his children for their summer visit. As her remarks on the subject of John Knightley's comportment and incomprehensible use of legal terminology would have fallen into the category of mild complaint, her husband's presence naturally stood in the way of the pursuit of this topic. Emma did on occasion wonder whether married life was destined to be a succession of captured confidences with friends.— For there was much to do with the running of the considerable estate of Donwell, and with arrangements for the entertainment of guests, which Mr. Knightley, after thirty-eight years as a bachelor, dictated without a thought to his young wife. Emma had frequent recourse to Mrs. Weston, and on occasion to Harriet Martin, when she felt the need to voice her opinions on the running of a household; and by so doing her own sense of superiority was restored.

"It is delightfully cool in here," remarked Mrs. Weston as she was shown to a chair in the parlour; but the manner in which her eyes roamed the bare walls of the room betrayed her continuing interest in Emma's covering them with the papers enclosed in the letter from Frank. Indeed, when John Knightley came in, and both brothers went to sit with a plan of the outlying land at Donwell, a portion of which was to be enclosed in the near future, Mrs. Weston could not forbear returning to the subject; and with a flourish she pulled a letter from her bag.

"Why does Frank take an interest in papers and the like?" enquired Emma, and she stifled a yawn. For she did not wish Mr. Knightley to hear talk of renovations: he was inclined to misunderstand when talk of altering Donwell came up; and had on two occasions berated Emma for speaking of them behind his back. It seemed Mr. Knightley had an idea that wives were intent on ruining their husbands' homes; and for all Emma's protestations that she was content for the old Abbey to remain exactly as it had always been, he clearly did not in the slightest believe her.

"I am not speaking of the papers," said Mrs. Weston,

as she pulled a letter from her bag and from it laid out squares of gaudy paper on the stone table, as if with the intention of distracting Mr. Knightley and his brother from the real purpose of her walking up to the Abbey from Randalls today. "It is a matter of an awkwardness, dear Emma—" And here Mrs. Weston unfolded the letter from Mr. Weston's son and read from it aloud.

"I shall be with you the seventeenth July," recited Mrs. Weston. "That is tomorrow, Emma. I am most distressed it should be the very same day—"

John Knightley rose from his seat at the far end of the parlour and approached his brother's wife and Mrs. Weston with a smile and a courtly bow. Emma smiled up at him, but, as she had increasingly to own, she did so with the effort of concealing her annoyance. For John Knightley, in the two years he had been a widower, had developed a ponderous manner, along with a habit of addressing all in his vicinity as if they sought counsel before taking the matter in hand to court. He had espoused his work, now his wife was gone: Emma felt the lack of her sister very sorely on the occasions of Mr. Knightley's brother's visit to the Abbey. The presence of the five children, Emma's nephews and nieces just as they were Mr. Knightley's, did not entirely alleviate the nuisance which Emma privately felt John Knightley had become.

"My dear Emma." As Emma had waited on him to

do, Mr. Knightley's brother stood very solemn by the tall chair where she sat facing Mrs. Weston. There was little doubt that a matter of some gravity was about to be broached; though whether the subject was trivial or important, John Knightley invariably attached the same weight to it.

"I am informed there may be thunder tonight," was the offering which Emma and Mrs. Weston finally received. "But all the evidence points to the contrary. There is none of that stillness in the air. A breeze comes as witness to other intentions on the part of the coming night. And tomorrow may be hot but still as fresh as today. What is your considered opinion, Emma? Mrs. Weston, you may give testimony after, and I shall examine both."

Mrs. Weston, who did not meet Emma's eye, declared the day innocent of thunderous intent. She thought it would not rain tomorrow, either; which was to be thanked for, as Mr. Frank Churchill came from Yorkshire tomorrow, and there it rained, or so it was said, very frequently.

Emma, who had declined to reply to the lawyer, saw that he looked at her askance.

"It is very uncertain, what the weather will do *here*," she said in a mild tone which failed to deceive her husband, who strolled from the end of the room and smiled at the assembled party. "But there are dreadful tempests in Weymouth – so Miss Bates informed James yesterday when he went there, for I thought to save her the walk up here in this heat."

"You did well to instruct him to take the basket of comestibles to Miss Bates before she could fatigue herself by walking to the Abbey," said Mr. Knightley; and Emma, who liked his praise, blushed on receiving it. "But how can Miss Bates know of Weymouth? She does not intend to go to the sea with old Mrs. Bates not likely to last out the summer, I daresay?"

"That would be culpable indeed!" said John Knightley, who proceeded to tuck his thumbs under his armpits and stride the room as if conducting a prosecution for the Crown. "I cannot imagine that Miss Bates would abandon her mother in these circumstances, notwithstanding the attentions of Mr. Perry and his good wife. No, Miss Bates would be tried by public opinion and I fear she would not be acquitted, were she to gallivant to the seaside at this critical juncture. Is that not so, brother George?"

"Nobody suggests that Miss Bates gallivants to the seaside!" Emma cried out in exasperation. For it was the case that John Knightley, since the demise of the sensible Isabella, appeared to have lost the power of discrimination between one person and another. Actions and evidence of them were all. "No, she has received a letter from her niece. Jane Fairfax is at Weymouth. She is in charge of Mrs. Smallridge's children; they board on the seafront; and Miss Bates's excitement lies solely in the fact that Jane travels here at this moment. Mrs. Smallridge comes to visit her friend Mrs. Elton at the Vicarage; and quite unexpectedly she has commanded the governess to bring the children to Highbury, to pass the rest of the summer here."

"It is that which I tried to tell you," said Mrs. Weston in a low voice as John Knightley demanded proof of Miss Fairfax's journey and Mrs. Smallridge's identity. "That is the awkwardness, Emma. Jane Fairfax and Frank Churchill will be here together, after four years – since the jilt – it is most reprehensible, do not you agree?"

Mr. Knightley, when he had attempted to answer the most detailed of his brother's questions, observed that the day showed no sign of growing cooler, and that an unpleasantly warm evening lay ahead for them at Donwell Abbey. "Come, let us all walk down to the stream. I need to remind Robert Martin to set more traps for moles; they are up everywhere by the vegetables. Come, Emma – Mrs. Weston, you will join us, I trust?"

There was little point in denying Mr. Knightley when he wished for a walk; and no wish on Emma's part to do so, for he generally went about the place alone, from habit.

They proceeded all four down the lime walk, exclaiming at the pleasantness of the shade; and had it not been for John Knightley, the subject of the unfortunate conjunction of Mr. Churchill and Miss Fairfax would not have been repeated.

"I recall Miss Fairfax as most reserved, a quality which is of particular merit to members of my profession," said John Knightley as the little party arrived at the boundary fence and looked down at the clear waters of the stream. "Does she not play the pianoforte remarkably well, also?"

Emma, holding Mrs. Weston's arm, squeezed it. "Indeed, Miss Fairfax is as reserved and as fine a player on the pianoforte as it is possible to be," she said, and looked up gravely at John Knightley; though his brother, who knew his Emma too well, was quick to shake his head at her.

Robert Martin, emerging from the Abbey Mill farmhouse on the bank across the stream, lifted his hat to them.

"You gave your word, Emma," said Mr. Knightley; but, along with Mrs. Weston, he smiled. "You are a married woman, my dear, and you have forsworn the meddling and matchmaking which you indulged in as a girl, have you not, Emma?"

Robert Martin, fording the stream and coming up towards them, put an end to the conversation. Mr.

Knightley went off with him to the terrain infested by moles, and John Knightley's children, in search of their aunt and uncle, ran up.

Mrs. Weston and Emma, however, pondered the coming days both in silence and aloud; though Mrs. Weston's opinion, that Jane Fairfax would never find John Knightley to her liking; and Emma's decision, which was that John Knightley and Jane Fairfax deserved each other exactly, were judgements each friend found wise to keep to herself.

2

Harriet Smith had been the subject of Emma's matchmaking attentions before her marriage to the farmer Robert Martin; yet despite this, she was not quick to understand the musings of her friend. Seeing Emma at the end of the lime walk, she had walked up in response to her beckoning, and the two ladies, having said farewell to Mrs. Weston, walked the mile to Hartfield, where arrangements were to be made for John Knightley's children. Emma in her talk interspersed her very natural concerns for the educational future of Henry and John and their younger siblings George, Bella and little Emma with speculation on the marital prospects of Jane Fairfax, so suddenly announced to be coming amongst them.

"It is a great pity that Frank Churchill acted as he did! I thought from the time he went to London to have his hair cut, that he had a frivolity in his nature which would serve poor Jane very ill. Did not you, Harriet?"

Harriet, who recalled only the painful misunderstanding of Emma's attempt to marry *her* to Mr. Weston's son while she had been busily engaged in falling in love with Mr. Knightley, blushed and said nothing. Had she so wished, Harriet could have found herself unpleasantly reminded of Emma's mis-matches at every turn of the road, and by the sight of any tree or flower; and sometimes, as she admitted only privately, she was made utterly downcast by the view of the church spire from the road (her infatuation with Mr. Elton) or a crowd of people outside the Crown (the dance where she had been rescued by Emma's gallant squire and had been foolish enough to fancy he loved her). On this occasion, and as ever, she said nothing; a silence taken by Emma as concurrence in her pronouncement on the character of Frank Churchill.

"Poor Jane!" said Emma again, when she had enquired of Harriet whether she had asked Mrs. Wells to bring pies to the school, so the children could eat there and become accustomed to their new surroundings before lessons began. To this, Harriet, whose soft blue eyes seldom left Emma's face as she talked, replied in the affirmative, and her friend and mentor was able to continue thinking aloud.

"John Knightley has been so very courageous since the sad loss of his wife, Harriet. Do not you think so? I believe he thinks of poor Isabella night and day; more even than I do, for she married and went to live in London when I was still so young. And, as Papa used to complain so, she never had time to come to Hartfield for longer than a few nights at a time! Little wonder her health was not strong – I speak like my father, I know – I am like him, so Mr. Knightley informs me, in more ways than I know. But I am not like Isabella; she was, as Mr. Knightley also says and everyone agrees, very like *me*!"

Harriet was out of her depth here, and paused on the road. A cloud of dust on this hot July day showed a carriage coming behind them at a good rate; the white dust rose into the air and was borne ahead, causing Emma to sneeze.

"Why, that is Mrs. Elton, and she will refer to the fact that she is out in her barouche-landau for a very special purpose," said Emma, laughing, for she was good-natured enough to recover from her sneezing fit and have little concern for streaming eyes and a ruined appearance. "She will say she brings red currant tarts and muffins to the poor orphans, Harriet, mark my words!"

Harriet, who had only just begun to understand that Jane Fairfax and John Knightley were to be married by Emma whether they liked it or no, stood back from the edge of the road as the carriage drew up. It was indeed the barouche-landau; Mrs. Elton sat in the back in great magnificence, in a purple satin dress looped and criss-crossed by brocade ribbons; at her side was an un-pleasant-looking woman, whose thin mouth went down at the corners and whose eyes appeared to travel at an unusual speed from side to side.

"Allow me to introduce Mrs. Smallridge," said Mrs. Elton, as she extended a hand from the carriage. Emma – followed by Harriet – had no choice but to receive her handshake in this way. "Mrs. Smallridge and I are out to explore – this is her first time at Highbury – how we loved expeditions when we were in Bristol, did we not, Alicia? And now – just as I sought to explain that two weddings and a funeral take up all the time of my *caro sposo* at present – that we cannot even once repeat the pleasure of a picnic at Box Hill but must remain close to home – we come across Knightley on our drive. And Knightley offers the chance of a boating party; it is to be on a lake at the extreme edges of his extensive estates – yours of course also, dear Mrs. Knightley—"

Emma showed by her frown and withdrawal to a part of the road where she might continue walking with Harriet, that she would no longer participate in this conversation. With a curt farewell she walked on, Harriet following as she was bound to do.

"It vexes me very much that Mrs. Elton should consider it acceptable to refer to my husband as 'Knightley'," said she crossly; and as always when in the company of Harriet, chiefly to herself. "How dare she indulge in such familiarity? There certainly shall be no boating party; I cannot think what lake she means, in any case; I have lived my life here and I have never seen a lake."

Harriet put forward that Mr. Knightley had jested, in order to give amusement to Emma on her return from Hartfield. But the spirits of the two friends were soon lowered once more by finding on arrival at the house which once had been home to Emma and her father Mr. Woodhouse, that Mrs. Elton's barouche-landau stood outside. A sound of voices engaged in the reciting of poetry emanated from the drawing-room, through a French window wide open in the heat of the day. As Emma and Harriet approached across the grass, the recitation faltered and stopped. Bella, who was the elder of John Knightley's two daughters, came to the window and looked out with an enquiring expression at her aunt. In the background, and clearly demonstrating her desire to be of service to Mrs. Elton, stood the children's governess Miss Whynne, brought by John Knightley from London.

"Whatever is going on?" demanded Emma, who was quite pale by now at the sight of the Vicar's wife in command of the drawing-room where once she had sat long evenings with her father. It was a room which, like the sites marked for Harriet's painful memories, would never be free of associations for her. "Why are you doing lessons with Mrs. Elton? Why did you not wait for me?"

"Mrs. Elton brought us pies – and muffins—" The child, who was no more than ten years old, became confused, and blushed scarlet. "I did not know, Aunt Emma—"

Mrs. Elton came to the window, Mrs. Smallridge following behind her. "My dear Mrs. Knightley, you must forgive our visiting the little school here – we are much taken with education, as you may be aware: why, Alicia has her hands full with training Miss Fairfax to reach some level of accuracy with her French verbs! There is nothing worse than a governess who is slovenly with her grammar, do not you agree, Mrs. Knightley?"

Emma, who found herself still speechless at the sight of her nephews and nieces munching on the charity from the Vicarage, said nothing and turned on her heel. It was left to Harriet to bid farewell for the second time to Mrs. Elton and Mrs. Smallridge, who stood framed in the open window as if about to commence a theatrical production of their own devising.

"Mrs. Elton treats my poor sister's children like

orphans," cried Emma, once the shrubberies of Hartfield were left behind and the road to Donwell Abbey embarked upon. "It was I who determined that Hartfield should not lie empty since my marriage; I who wished to try as an experiment the educating of my nephews and nieces; and I who suggested to John Knightley that we commence gently, with only Miss Whynne, while Mrs. Weston might include her own little Adelaide in the plan, should it prove successful. And Mrs. Elton has the impudence to sweep in, with tarts—"

"John Knightley certainly has need of a wife," said Harriet, who had now grasped the gist of Emma's earlier thoughts. "The children need a mother, however much time and attention you may give them, Mrs. Knightley. Oh, they do!"

Emma walked on in silence, leaving Harriet to regurgitate their conversations on the walk; and to wonder, if Emma disliked Mrs. Elton referring to the squire of Donwell Abbey as Knightley, why she had not once heard his wife call him George.

But this, like so many of her revered Emma's foibles, was quite beyond Harriet to imagine. For the present, Mrs. Elton's insufferable bounty at Hartfield was enough to occupy them both.

3

An entire evening was to be got through before Emma could pay a visit to Miss Bates, and thus ascertain that her niece was indeed just arrived at Highbury. A dinner could then be put forward as a pleasant occasion for all three: Miss Bates; her mother, old Mrs. Bates – who, as Emma did not like to admit to herself, was not so frequent a recipient of the Knightleys' hospitality as she had been at Hartfield; and Jane Fairfax herself, who was by now as good as wed to Mr. Knightley's brother in Emma's mind as if Mr. Elton had pronounced the couple man and wife but a day or so ago at the altar.

Emma had never liked Jane Fairfax. The reserve and caution exhibited by the beautiful young woman at the time of her secret engagement to Frank Churchill had been repulsive to one so openly desirous of controlling the lives of others as Emma Woodhouse; and Mr. Knightley's frank accusation that Emma's dislike of one so much less fortunate than she originated in an unconscious recognition of Jane's superior accomplishments, had done little to increase her fondness for one she had learnt to see as a rival.

But now!— now all was different. Emma had imagination enough to know the life of a governess as drudgery with no end but an unvisited grave; and sufficient compassion, as one who had (albeit for a very brief period indeed) fancied herself in love with Frank, to pity the duped maiden, abandoned almost at the church, and in a season which saw the triumph of her own wedding to Mr. Knightley. (That Harriet, so frequently seen as wife to various unwilling suitors, had also married in that fair September four years ago, must have brought sadness to the jilted bride.)

Emma had every opportunity now, to make recompense for the ill will she had borne the young woman who had, unbeknownst to Highbury, been keeper of the nefarious Frank Churchill's affections. Frank, as he had done in all the years since his adoption by his aunt, Mrs. Churchill, obeyed her: in death, even as in life, as it transpired, for a Will which dictated the joining of the Churchill family with another as illustrious in Yorkshire had caused a breach of the engagement with Jane Fairfax, apparently with little scruple on his part. Mrs. Elton, like a shark that waits in waters bloodied by a fall, swam up with her repeated offer of an excellent situation for Jane. Mrs. Smallridge waited in hope for Miss Fairfax to take charge of the education of her children. The die was cast.

To elevate the poor creature from the misery of her circumstance – to see her married to a man infinitely superior in fortune and rank to the husbands of Mrs. Elton and Mrs. Smallridge put together – this would be a fine deed on Emma's part. She was already halfway to housing the newly-bonded couple at Hartfield – did the place not begin a fresh life as a school? Would not Jane and John Knightley find themselves happy to have all his children educated there, and any of theirs as they came along? Was Miss Fairfax not already a proficient teacher?— when Mr. Knightley, seeing from the end of the dining-table that she was distracted with her own thoughts, called out to her laughingly:

"Emma my dear, you appear too serious by half! Can you not share your reflections with us? It seems they are momentous indeed."

Emma blushed, for John Knightley, who had been speaking with that tireless monotony that had come to particularise his address of the past year or so, ceased his argument and stared directly across the table at her. For a moment, as Emma had no choice but to acknowledge, there came a doubt as to whether even Miss Fairfax, with her total lack of independence, would countenance a lifetime with a man such as John Knightley.

"I think of a dinner, to which we invite Miss Bates," said Emma in reply, once she had pushed this unwelcome thought to the back of her mind. "It is an age since she came here – and old Mrs. Bates shall come too. She is partial to minced chicken and oyster patties. Dear papa would never permit old Mrs. Bates to eat her fill: 'She should not partake so generously, at her age' – do you recall what a business there was, for me to smuggle extra helpings on to Mrs. Bates's platter?"

"And will there be others at this occasion?" said Mr. Knightley gravely. It was clear to Emma that he had not been for one moment taken in. "My brother John will be included in the party, no doubt? Have you not more amusing company to add to your list of Miss Bates and her aged mother? Mr. and Mrs. Elton, perhaps? They invite us to the Vicarage frequently enough. Surely you must have them in mind."

Emma blushed with vexation. She knew Mr. Knightley teased her, and was glad of John Knightley's interruption at this point. "My dear Emma," said John Knightley, taking out a monocle as he spoke and consulting a candlestick at the centre of the table, as if demanding that it bear witness to his deliberations.

"You must be aware that I prefer to weigh the pros and cons of a situation before committing myself fully to it. In this case, we examine a dinner party at Donwell Abbey. The pros, naturally, include the presence of your good self, and my brother George. But, with your permission, I already have that pleasure on numerous other occasions. The cons consist of the fact, as I am loath to testify, that Miss Bates does not present her evidence at all clearly. Indeed, when she speaks I am hard pressed not to put an end to it there and then!"

So saying, John Knightley brought down his fork loudly on the table, as if it had been a gavel. Emma shrank back in annoyance; Mr. Knightley, from his more distant chair, laughed.

"If Miss Bates's niece Miss Fairfax is come to visit Highbury," Emma began demurely.

"Ah, now we have it," roared Mr. Knightley, "a lovely young lady may well tip the balance here for brother John! What say you, brother? A Miss Fairfax who plays the pianoforte superbly; has a delicacy of complexion remarked on in every place she visits, and can paint and recite poetry most affectingly. Will this change your view of our little dinner at Donwell Abbey?"

"I am not in the habit of conversing with young ladies," came the reply; and Emma, seeing her brother-in-law was confused by what he took to be a secret between her and Mr. Knightley, bit her lip and refrained from upbraiding her husband on his rough manners. There was still enough real sadness left in her at the loss of Isabella not to reproach herself with setting up a party for John Knightley and Jane Fairfax. She almost began to wish she had not thought of it in the first place. But the feeling did not last long; and Miss Whynne knocking at the door and coming in to say little Emma cried, and should they send for Mr. Perry as her head was so hot, soon decided her to continue with her design. John Knightley's children, as Harriet Martin had observed, were sorely in need of a mother. Emma liked to think she could undertake their education over the duration of the summer at Hartfield. But she could not be responsible for them, for the rest of her life. That would be intolerable.

"We have still our backgammon contest to conclude," remarked Mr. Knightley in a milder tone when Emma reappeared from the nurseries with the news that her younger niece was already asleep again, calmed by milk and by the attentions of her aunt. "You were winning, Emma – but I wager brother John will beat you before the evening is out. Will you play?"

Emma, knowing this to be a conciliatory gesture, agreed; but by showing reserve in her acceptance she demonstrated her determination to go ahead with her party; while Mr. Knightley's frequent glances across the board manifested in equal measure his continuing disapproval of Emma's matchmaking tendencies. These, as she had reminded him, had ended with the only successful match to have come about: that between herself and him; and that it had taken place by accident was a fact of which Mr. Knightley constantly reminded her.

4

There had not been an occasion on the previous evening for Emma to bring up with Mr. Knightley the vexed subject of Mrs. Elton and her visit to Hartfield. Before mounting into the chaise which would take her down to Miss Bates the next morning she therefore stopped him as he crossed the hall of Donwell Abbey and demanded he put an end to such indiscretions on the part of the Vicar's wife.

"Mrs. Elton – Augusta, as she would have me address her, though I absolutely refuse to do so – has the want of delicacy to take her charity to our family! I insist that you speak directly to Mr. Elton. She takes with her a stranger, a Mrs. Smallridge, who eyes the furniture that was in the private ownership of dear Papa— and, I may remind you, is mine! They are no more than vulgar trippers; and familiar with it, with Mrs. Elton's 'Mr. K' and 'Knightley' – does it not annoy you? – can you not demand that I am left alone to supervise my little school in the house I lived in, and loved, from childhood?"

"Beloved Emma, calm yourself," said Mr. Knightley, for he perceived that she was overcome at the insult she fancied paid to her years with Mr. Woodhouse; and thus to her name and home. "But I may say, whether you like to hear it or not, that Mrs. Elton's sentiments do not differ one jot from your own. There – you must forgive me, my dear. My anxieties over the prospect of my wife at the head of a school are, however, of a more serious nature than whether or not impediments to her self-esteem come in the shape of muffins proffered to the children there."

"What are you saying?" cried Emma, who was quick to suspect censure from Mr. Knightley, accustomed as she had been from her earliest years to receive and ponder a lecture or a snub from him.

"I say that Mrs. Elton brings her charity from the church when she goes out, seeking to do good. Yours comes from the squire: that is all."

"So there is no distinction between us," said Emma bitterly. "I did not think I would hear this."

"No, now Emma," said Mr. Knightley, laughing. "I shall go further, whether you threaten to banish me from your heart or not. I shall say that you must take care not to give the impression to the children that they are settled here permanently in the school. The experiment may not succeed. Brother John may wish to remove his family to London; and it will be Christmas before they come here again. As it is, he spoke of Miss Whynne in the highest terms only yesterday, saying he would entrust the younger members of his family to her anywhere; while Henry and John must go away to boarding school. If I can assist them to do so, that is," he added in a lower tone.

"So your brother has already complained at my teaching methods," said Emma, who did not hear the grave note which had entered his voice. She was in a glow, from the anger she felt against Mr. Knightley and John; and for a minute or so she determined that there should be no Mrs. John Knightley: he did not deserve Miss Fairfax; and the dark head which Frank Churchill had once wished to crown with his mother's jewels should remain ungarnished by those gems of old Mrs. Knightley's which had not been particularly reserved for *her*.

"My brother thinks the world of you, Emma," said Mr. Knightley. "But it is for him to decide how his children shall be educated, and how he shall pass the remainder of his life. You know to what I allude, I have little doubt. John has told me he has no wish to remarry.

You will do well to remember that, Emma."

"He may do as he pleases," said Emma crossly, mounting up into the chaise and taking the reins. Then, seeing a parcel on the floor of the vehicle, she pulled it up into her arms and sniffed it vigorously, before bursting into laughter. "You are sending a hindquarter of pork down to Miss Bates and her mother by this means? My goodness, Mr. Knightley, they will think me better than Mrs. Elton, if I appear so laden with your kindness. Miss Bates has not yet recovered from your gift of the last bushel of apples from Donwell; she had it from Mrs. Hodges that we had no apple pies or baked apples for the whole of the spring, due to your munificence. She and her mother will be overcome, I am sure!"

For all that Emma spoke in the bantering tone so frequently adopted by couples who have heard too much from each other over the years, be it praise or blame, her eyes brimmed with tears, and Mr. Knightley, seeing she was upset, came up to the carriage and laid his hand on the edge, fearing, it seemed, to go further and lay a finger on her. "I only wished to remind you that a man of five and thirty is capable of making his own decisions on the subject of his future wife, Emma. And John—"

At this point John Knightley came into view, his son George and a tall fishing-rod as accompaniment; and

Mr. Knightley looked away, displeased at the untimeliness of the interruption.

"Do they go to this famous lake, of which I have never heard you speak?" said Emma, recovering her spirits. For she loved Mr. Knightley; so she said to herself twenty times a day; and it had ever been his habit to find fault with her and to see the omissions in her heart which were in need of reparation and supply. She knew he loved *her*: he tried to curb his manner; but, as Emma told herself, the man she had married was as English as the Abbey, the climate, the very soil where Donwell stood. He was blunt; reserved; but in every way superior to a man who would have been more fulsome in his commendations and more lacking in the censure she knew herself on occasion to require.

So Emma told herself; but she knew, for all her faults, that she must be perfect. And secretly she believed Mr. Knightley found her so also.

"We were speaking of the lake," called Mr. Knightley in a voice that was distinctly jocular, to his brother. "Emma says she has never heard it talked of. You must explain, brother John, that it was on a part of our mother's land, let out on a lease and put in your name and only now returned to us; it is quite at the other extremity of the county."

"Yes, it was an interesting question of the escrow," John Knightley began; but Emma, unable to hide her desire not to hear of it, whipped up the horse and departed at a trot down the Abbey drive. If there was one subject she could not bear, it was land law and all its ramifications. The very idea of John Knightley discussing his mother's portion, and the land which he now inherited, was anathema to her. It was with all the greater determination that she hastened to Highbury to extend the dinner invitation. John Knightley and Jane Fairfax should marry as soon as possible; and Emma placed them already in a comfortable farmhouse at the other extremity of Surrey.

5

"I do not know what your opinion may be, Mrs. Weston," said Mr. Knightley, "of Emma's desire for a party at Donwell Abbey. She speaks of a dinner, but she will envisage larger numbers than our table can provide for. I believe she forgets we have company here already, in the form of my brother John; by the time she has invited the whole of Highbury, there will be no room to seat him anywhere."

"And I bring news of a swelling in our own ranks," said Mrs. Weston. "I came to the Abbey to inform you—"

"To inform Emma," said Mr. Knightley, his eyes still alight with merriment; for he could understand that

Mrs. Weston refused to refer to his allusions to his brother, and yet would not be able to refuse a discussion of it with him, if pressed. I was the last one she wanted to see, concluded Mr. Knightley with some satisfaction: she comes across the fields from Randalls to conspire with Mrs. Knightley and finds herself caught by the husband, while the wife goes by road to extend her invitations to Miss Bates and her niece.

Mrs. Weston had been acquainted with Mr. Knightley for close on twenty years; together they had witnessed the growing of Emma; and in conjunction had delighted in the developing maturity of that most wonderful specimen, a flower of young English womanhood without the want of riches, intelligence or looks. Mrs. Weston and Mr. Knightley were, in their own minds and without the slightest doubt, the cultivators and gardeners of Emma. For all that the past governess had found herself sad to miss her pupil – as she still did sometimes think her – on this occasion, there was nonetheless the comfort of comparing with Mr. Knightley the progress made by their protégée. He had frequently declared himself satisfied with the bride Emma had become, if he mourned her refusal to remove from Mrs. Hodges any of the responsibilities of cook or housekeeper. Mrs. Weston found Emma also much improved: her sole anxiety lay in the fear she might not propagate, in her own little daughter, the seeds of so faultless a bloom as

Emma. So, once she had comforted herself with the reassurance that Mr. Knightley was not in one of his teasing moods (if he was, she had not seen it), she settled for an exchange on the virtues of the girl she had raised and Mr. Knightley had watched over with care; and, having resigned herself to a lack of the company she liked best in the world, gave all she had to the concerns of Mr. Knightley.

"It grows ever hotter today," said he; and Mrs. Weston fancied he looked at her closely. "I shall provide lemonade for you, my dear Mrs. Weston, even if my nephews and nieces have guzzled the entire jug, and Mrs. Hodges must be asked for more. You must be fatigued, walking over the fields. And it is a pity you missed Emma. She goes to Miss Bates, to invite that good lady and her niece to this famous dinner here."

A servant came in, summoned by Mr. Knightley's bell, and lemonade was asked for.

"It is certain," continued Mr. Knightley, "that Mr. Weston and your good self will be the next recipients of Emma's invitation to Donwell Abbey. I hope you might suggest to her that that will make for a sufficiency of guests – with Miss Bates, naturally; and her mother, for whom Emma has every receipt in readiness. Emma loves to spoil old Mrs. Bates, you know."

"Indeed!" replied Mrs. Weston, who knew as well as her companion that Emma forgot old Mrs. Bates at every possible opportunity, and was only reminded by a sense of reproach at herself, of the old lady's existence. It was also known to Mrs. Weston as well as it was to her host that the first reproach came inevitably from Mr. Knightley himself, to his wife; and that she cried in vexation each time it came, at her neglect of the one member of Highbury society who lived in hope of the fricassée of veal – or of a slice of turkey that had not been cooked too far in advance of a Sunday (as happened on so many occasions that she and her daughter were presented with a bird), by reason of their lack of a larder to store it.

"This dinner at Donwell Abbey will more than compensate for past omissions," said Mrs. Weston. "But I fear Mr. Weston and I must decline your kind invitation, Mr. Knightley. It grieves me very much to say it: I do love to see Emma at the head of the table, a beacon of loveliness indeed!"

"But Emma will not wish to hold the dinner if you are not present," said Mr. Knightley, frowning. "Can we not settle on a day which is convenient to Randalls and the Abbey together? Surely it must be possible."

"It is not a question of a day," said Mrs. Weston, becoming flustered. "We are taken up over the next weeks, Mr. Knightley. The situation was not expected. Please forgive us."

The lemonade made an entrance; and when the

servant had gone, Mr. Knightley set himself to changing Mrs. Weston's mind. After a few attempts the truth came out, and the good Mrs. Weston, blushing, asked pardon once more at the inconvenience caused at the Abbey by the arrival of not one but two young men, at her husband's house.

"Two, Mrs. Weston? It is certain the table here would not stretch to such a party.— For they must be invited.— Yet I may ask of my brother that he goes to dine at the Crown that evening, I suppose.— Yes, my dear madam, I do credit you with solving our little problem most magnificently!"

Mrs. Weston, not for the first time since the beginning of her long acquaintanceship with Mr. Knightley, found it in her to criticise him. He was dogmatic; petty; she did not wish her Emma to be subjected to further strictures on the capacity of the dining-table at Donwell Abbey. He has been too long a bachelor, thought Mrs. Weston. It did not occur to her that the aim of the worthy squire was simply to prevent John Knightley meeting Miss Bates's niece. There was no reason for her to suppose it. Though she was soon to come to that realisation.

"So who are these two young men?" continued Mr. Knightley, and this time with a magisterial air. "I can guess one, certainly. He is Mr. Weston's son Frank Churchill. Here is a good reason why Miss Bates cannot bring along her niece Miss Fairfax to dinner on the same evening. It would be most awkward, would it not, Mrs. Weston, for a young woman who has been jilted to come up against her jilt, at our table? Emma cannot have thought carefully before planning out this occasion. She cannot!"

"The other is Frank's brother-in-law, Captain Brocklehurst," said Mrs. Weston. "It was a decision made at the very last minute, to come down from Yorkshire and visit the family – the other part of the family – into which his sister has married. I am not at all sure there are towels in the linen cupboard to cover his stay," added Mrs. Weston; and her doing so might have indicated to a more sensible listener the anxieties entertained at this costly and unforeseen visit. Mr. Knightley, however, remained in his wing chair, slightly tilted back, with fingertips pressed together; and for a moment Mrs. Weston saw his lawyer brother in his pose, and in the judicial manner in which he appeared to examine the information she had been brought to offer him.

"Captain Brocklehurst, eh?" As if tired of the subject, Mr. Knightley swung forward and rose to his feet. Mrs. Weston was always to see him as smaller than she remembered, in his boots. But his position, and the gravity with which he conducted himself, made up for the slight deficiency of stature.

"Let us permit this dinner to work out its own problems," said he; "and accept my sincere apologies,

Mrs. Weston, for airing my concerns over Emma – for this is what they are.— I wish to hear your opinions on her happiness; on the school she both tends and neglects; and on the important matter of whether you find her dabbling in making matches again; for she gave her word she would do no such thing!"

But Mrs. Weston, who now understood the purpose of Mr. Knightley's attitude towards her, would only say she found Emma's efforts with the education of her nephews and nieces admirable in the extreme, while no ostensible sign of a return to matchmaking had been noted by Mrs. Weston in the course of earlier conversations.

"Emma wishes to introduce her brother to the neighbourhood, that is all," said Mrs. Weston; and her tone was soothing. "She hopes one day, I have no doubt, that he will find happiness in love, as she has—"

"Has she, Mrs. Weston?" said Mr. Knightley, and his eagerness, being so evident to Mrs. Weston, caused her to look away. "I proclaimed, did I not, as many as five years ago, that I wished to see Emma in love. Do you see this, Mrs. Weston? Speak freely, I implore you!"

Mrs. Weston, who made much of picking up her bag and searching for her spectacles on the table, was at last ready to give a reply. "Oh I do, Mr. Knightley. Emma is very much in love!"

And with these words Mrs. Weston excused herself;

she had two young men at Randalls, and the butcher's boy had yet to come, when she set out.—

Mr. Knightley, escorting her to the door, could be perceived to return to his chair and sit a long time very still.

6

 ray take care, Mrs. Knightley, ours is
rather a dark staircase – Oh, it is too
kind . . . a hindquarter of pork – I do not
know what my mother will say – take care I do beg of
you, that you do not hit your foot at the turning. I am
quite at a loss – my mother – you will see she is a trifle
unwell, but she will be restored by the pork! Even more
succulent than the meat dear Mr. Woodhouse would
send down.— Oh, you are all too kind.— I do not mean
to disparage your late father, Oh, goodness no. Very."

Emma could not walk into Miss Bates's little sitting-
room without smiling at the memory of Mr. Knightley
calling up to the windows, on the occasion of delivering
a bushel of apples to daughter and mother. She had

wondered since whether she had come to recognise her feelings for him on that day. For Mr. Knightley liked to keep his charity a secret; and Emma had been unable to prevent herself from comparing it with her own activities in visiting the poor, all of which were well known in the village.

Mrs. Bates slumbered by the fireplace; but soon woke when Emma's presence was announced. There was no sign of Jane Fairfax, however, and questions as to her whereabouts were met by Miss Bates with some show of hesitation.

"I do not believe there are families as distinguished as Mrs. Smallridge's family in all of England. Only the Sucklings and the Bragges come anywhere near her . . . well perhaps the Sucklings can be called superior, if only by reason of the extent of their park; but Mrs. Elton assures me Jane is so very happy. So very. In a house which is only four miles from Mrs. Elton's old home. Maple Grove. And on the occasion of Mrs. Elton's going for a visit, she saw dear Jane several times! Can you imagine? Jane most satisfied. Candles in the school-room. She wants for nothing, dear Mrs. Knightley, I can assure you. Last year she was in Norfolk in the summer, with the three children. Three little girls. Is it not delightful? This year she has been at Weymouth; and all arranged with an idea to her happiness, for Colonel and Mrs. Campbell are at Weymouth, you know, and Jane's great friends Mr. and Mrs. Dixon visiting them there. Can you give credence to anything so agreeable as that?"

"How shall we salt the pork?" enquired Mrs. Bates from her seat by the fire. The good lady had now placed her spectacles on her nose, to examine the hindquarter; and after pronouncing it excellent, she fell off to sleep again.

"My poor mother does not enjoy this heat," said Miss Bates. "She is for ever. And you are. It is so kind of you. Indeed."

Emma saw that Miss Bates was more confused than usual, today; she felt with a pang of self-reproach that she had not visited her in a long time. Mr. Woodhouse would also have gone more often to see that Miss Bates and her mother were in good health. Now, from the appearance and speech of Miss Bates, her mother was declining sadly, and the daughter was distraught by the imminent loss of a loved parent.

"I trust Mrs. Bates is well," said Emma, who was at last prevailed upon to sit down, and was able to look around her. The pianoforte was gone; she saw this with a pang. Poor Jane Fairfax! She would not play for her own amusement again.

"Mother is doing excellently well for her years," replied Miss Bates. "You do not ask in any spirit of true concern, do you, dear Mrs. Knightley?"

Before Emma – abashed by this sudden revelation on Miss Bates's part of the sad truth of the long neglect on the part of the mistress of Donwell Abbey of the two ladies most esteemed in Highbury (their poverty, constant kindnesses to all and inability to cause harm to anyone had earned them this accolade) – could discover a way to evade the directness of Miss Bates's question, the stream of utterance went on.

"You are cordially invited to take tea or dinner with us. Yes. Mr. Knightley and yourself. You will, I hope, Mrs. Knightley. It would be so great an honour. Yes. Yes. And Mr. and Mrs. Cole have asked a hundred times. No, maybe it is five or six times, if they may invite you. They do not dare approach Donwell Abbey. 'But Mrs. Knightley – dear Emma – is a great friend of mine,' I said to Mrs. Cole. 'I shall ask her to meet you here. Then you may go ahead with your invitation.' As for Mr. Knightley, he keeps my mother in apples, you know. Oh yes, even if he has to go without, he ensures we are stuffed. Yes. But Jane is not a great apple-eater and we do not need such quantities. They rot and they stink – oh, I beg your pardon, Mrs. Knightley – but we are in such close quarters here—"

"Where is Miss Fairfax?" cried Emma, for she was determined to insert a word while Miss Bates paused for breath. "Mrs. Weston informed us she came here. We assumed she would stay in her old home, that her situation with Mrs. Smallridge would permit it, if only for a short time. Is she delayed at Weymouth still?"

"Delayed?" answered Miss Bates. "If only she were, dear Emma – if I may, my dear, if I may. No, Jane is out walking. It is most unfortunate. No sooner has she arrived here – she brings a friend, you know."

"A friend?" said Emma, frowning. She saw her numbers for the dinner grow too great for Mr. Knightley to permit it to take place. There would be an altercation over the walnut table in the morning-room, which Mr. Knightley's mother had sat at, with her sewing. For some reason this piece could not be moved to the dining-room without a great deal of fuss on the part of Mr. Knightley.

"Jane does not stay here," said Miss Bates. "She is with Mrs. Elton. The good vicar's wife has Mrs. Small-ridge as guest. Mrs. Smallridge insists on Jane staying with the children. There. There. It cannot be helped. We are so very fortunate, my dear."

Emma was appalled at this lack of kindness towards a poor governess. In her agitation she rose, and with the suddenness of her movement, the floorboards of the old house trembled, causing Mrs. Bates to wake and her spectacles to slide from footstool to floor.

"Please forgive me!" And, retrieving the spectacles Emma noted with horror that the frames had cracked and were in need of putting together again before they could be of use to the wearer. "Oh, Mrs. Bates, I will ensure these are seen to as soon as I possibly can!" cried Emma.

But a closer inspection of the old lady proved to be of more concern than a pair of broken spectacles. For, whatever Miss Bates might say on the subject of her mother's health, old Mrs. Bates did not appear well at all. Her breathing was slow and quiet, but irregular and punctuated with little gasps: that she had made an outstanding effort to comment on the gift of pork accounted only too well for the sleep which had immediately succeeded it.

"I had hoped to invite you and your mother to dinner," said Emma as Mrs. Bates lapsed once more into a comatose state; and she blamed herself as she spoke for a lack of delicacy in putting her dinner always at the head of every subject, for it was evident that old Mrs. Bates could not go out in company and that her daughter must stay and care for her. Nevertheless, Emma persevered: if she could not bring news home that Miss Bates and her mother came to Donwell Abbey, then Jane Fairfax must be counted on. And it was Jane she chased. There was no question of Miss Bates marrying John Knightley.— These thoughts flashed across Emma's mind, but she censured herself for them.

"We shall be delighted to come," said Miss Bates, to Emma's surprise. "Why, my mother cannot forget – last summer, was it already? – that Mrs. Hodges did so well with the dessert—"

"And Miss Fairfax," said Emma. "Will her friend mind, if she does not accompany her to Donwell on this occasion? There is not room at the dining-room table, now we have Mr. Knightley's brother in the house."

"Mrs. Hodges is most accomplished," said Miss Bates. "She made a perfect fart."

Emma, still standing by the fireside of the little room, glanced at Miss Bates in consternation.

"A raspberry tart," said Miss Bates, as Emma made her farewells with all the good manners required on the occasion of the departure of the squire's wife from a simple abode. "Be careful at the turning, dear Mrs. Knightley. Yes, Mother and I will be delighted to accept. But of Jane I cannot give any assurances. Watch how you go, Mrs. Knightley!"

And, as Emma let herself from the narrow hall she distinctly heard, from above and in Miss Bates's un-mistakable tones, the word "Bollocks!"

7

*E*mma left the Bates household confused and un-happy. She knew she must report to Mr. Knightley that the health of old Mrs. Bates was certain to render any kind of a party being attended by her at Donwell Abbey an impossibility; and at the same time she knew Mr. Knightley well enough to imagine him declaring, with no little triumph, that the dinner need now not take place. It might be simpler – and Emma thought this with some unease – to avoid any reference to the old lady's condition: if the daughter (and here Emma refused to think of Miss Bates's own state, both physical and mental: the conclusion might prove too shocking and distressing) declared her mother well enough to go out in company, then surely that should be good enough for the hosts? It was hard indeed to decide which to do. In the meantime, Mrs. Bates's spectacles were in pieces: it was Emma's duty, without a doubt, to find a man with some knowledge of putting them together again; and it was with considerable relief that Emma saw Mr. Perry walking up the street, his doctor's bag in one hand and the other waving genially at her as he came.

"My dear Mrs. Knightley! It is some weeks since I was last at the Abbey, and on that occasion it was to bring James better news of his daughter Hannah's prospects for recovery. You are all well, I trust?"

"Yes," replied Emma, who was here able to smile with a degree of complacency – for the coachman James, brought by her from Hartfield at the time of Mr. Woodhouse's death, had suffered agonies at the fever of his daughter Hannah, employed at Randalls; and Emma, just as much as Mr. Perry, had ministered to the sick girl with calf's foot jelly and the cold compresses advised by her father's old doctor. "We are in splendid health at Donwell Abbey. But—" and here Emma lowered her voice, so Mr. Perry, standing in the street, walked along several feet to hear her. "But I am just come from Miss Bates and her mother. I was most awkward, I stepped too fast on their shaky floor and a pair of spectacles were broken—"

"Do not fret," said Mr. Perry, and in his tones Emma

remembered the wrappings-up against the winter cold, at her father's house, and the measles and chicken-pox all attended by him, with Mrs. Weston in tow; and she smiled most entrancingly, once again. From the corner of her eye she could see a movement in the street, otherwise so quiet at midday, but she would not say, had she been demanded to think back on that time, that she had extended the smile a few seconds longer as a result of it.

"I have invited Mrs. Bates to dinner," said Emma simply – for she understood Mr. Perry still saw her as a child, with all the directness of her early years. "I must ask you, Mr. Perry, whether it is advisable for Mrs. Bates to go out.— Even if we make the meal begin and end at a much earlier hour. Can she survive the carriage ride, the excitement of company? It seems she sleeps, and wishes only to sleep more."

"Mrs. Bates is old," said Mr. Perry. As he spoke, Emma looked innocently along the street, and saw – she had been right to expect some curiosity on the part of the denizens of Highbury – two young men on horse-back who came at a leisurely pace down the length of the thoroughfare, and paused outside Ford's as if to look with the greatest seriousness into the shop window. "It is not Mrs. Bates who concerns me," said Mr. Perry. "No, I fear it is not, Mrs. Knightley."

Emma, who was now overtly occupied in examining

these arrivals in the village, seemed not to hear him. Instead, she burst out: "It is Frank Churchill! Indeed it is! I do not know why I show surprise at his being here. Mrs. Weston said he was coming, after all. But I suppose there have been many occasions in the past when Mr. Churchill's visit was earnestly expected, and he did not come. But here he is. And with him—"

"There will very likely be a rapid deterioration," pronounced Mr. Perry, who gave evidence of being a good deal less interested in the gentlemen on horseback than his companion. "There must be toleration – Mr. Knightley should be informed, if she is to be a guest in polite society. She would not object in the least to my warning you of this, dear Emma!"

The use of the childhood address brought Emma to her senses. She saw she had hardly heard a word of Mr. Perry's discourse – and he, a busy man, had only wished to answer her question with tact and accuracy. That he also observed the distracted state of the young woman whose position was unrivalled in Highbury and the surrounding country, was a distinct possibility. No more than wishing her, in those distant days at Hartfield, to expose herself to the vagaries of a thunderstorm, with its attendant risk of being struck by lightning – nor of permitting his little charge to run barefoot in the snow, however much she begged to – did Mr. Perry desire Emma Knightley to manifest her interest, before a growing number of people, in the visiting gentlemen in Highbury.

The reason for Emma's being unable to take her eyes away was quite plain: Frank Churchill, once considered the handsomest man in the small society formed by Randalls, Hartfield and the others of that important circle, was now surpassed – and by his comrade, the other equestrian come amongst them.

It must be Captain Brocklehurst, thought Emma; but, seeing Mr. Perry's eyes upon her, she did not put her conjecture into words. "So we are quite safe to proceed with our dinner at Donwell?" said Emma instead; and Mr. Perry, glad her intelligent gaze was now trained on him once more, continued with his assurances.

"You have nothing to fear, Mrs. Knightley. So long as the odd lapse – it is a concomitant of the disease, regrettably – does not offend anyone present. And I may be certain that all at Donwell Abbey will be as tolerant of what may at first appear to be remiss behaviour as you are – and as your late father, the esteemed Mr. Woodhouse was, dear Mrs. Knightley!"

It was usual for a mention of Mr. Woodhouse to bring a sigh to Emma's lips, even on occasion a tear to her eye; but as Frank Churchill and his companion dismounted and came towards her to present their compliments, Mr. Perry was able to observe only a heightening of colour in the cheeks of the mistress of Donwell Abbey; and, had he not known better, he would have diagnosed scarlet fever, or rubella at the very least.

"Mrs. Knightley, may I present my brother-in-law Captain Brocklehurst?"

Frank Churchill was bowing: he looked highly amused; and Emma for a moment wished him at the other end of the earth. She knew he knew her; or the worst side of her, at any rate, was known only too well, by the young man who had indulged in hypocrisy and deceit – in espionage and treachery – in order to disguise his engagement to Jane Fairfax by seeming to court Emma Woodhouse.

Emma held out her hand, but she did not look directly at the stranger. That Captain Brocklehurst should bring so powerful a reminder of Frank Churchill's further treachery – worse, far worse, in abandoning poor Jane at the church door, when news came by express of the conditions of his aunt's will, than a mere flirtation – was intolerable for poor Jane. And here they were, standing outside the house of Jane's aunt, no less!— where the jilted girl had been happy, the house she thought of as home, despite the kindness of Colonel and Mrs. Campbell, in rearing and educating her, which Miss Bates could never have afforded to do. It was shameful! But Captain Brocklehurst was quite the handsomest man – when Emma did at last raise her eyes to his – that she, or the village of Highbury, populous though it might increasingly be, had ever seen. He was taller than Frank; his hair was dark and very smooth; his features were of that perfect symmetry so seldom found in English men. Yet he had not a hint of the foreigner about him; and from the very first, his quiet and well-spoken words could do little other than charm, though in the politest possible way.

"I trust we shall all meet at Randalls," said Emma; and, as this came after a description almost vulgar in its fulsomeness, from Mr. Churchill, of the glories of Donwell Abbey, she could think well to herself that she had defended Jane Fairfax, and had not succumbed to the allure of the two young men.

Jane shall come to dinner. How right Mr. Knightley was to decry my wish to invite Mrs. Weston on the same evening, thought Emma; for the party rose once more in her mind, and the spectre of Jane, surrounded by hideous apparitions from a marriage which could never now take place, made her shudder at her thoughtless and impulsive intent. Of course Jane has gone out walking: wretched creature, she came from her obligations as governess on one of the scarce hours she has to herself, with the express intention of visiting her aunt and her aunt's mother. Then – learning Mr. Churchill was in the vicinity – dreading coming across him – and even more painful to her, the brother of the woman Mr. Churchill found easy, for reason of fifty thousand pounds, to marry – no, it is too horrible! But it is saved. I shall not invite Mr. Churchill to Donwell Abbey, and he may make of it what he likes!

Mr. Perry, who had been attempting to disengage himself from the group for some minutes announced in the firm tones of a busy medical man that he was on his way to visit the Bates household: he must be excused, but time this morning was short. "There is old John Abdy to see to," said Mr. Perry. "He will not last out the summer. His son John Abdy has applied several times to the parish council for relief – his sister, widowed, wishes to return to the family, but there is not money enough to make the barn habitable. She could care for her father, if she brought her children and lived there – but it is not to be."

"Mrs. Knightley will wave her magic wand, I have no doubt," said Frank Churchill, with a smile which Emma found odious in its desire to ingratiate. "Why, if I am not mistaken, old Abdy was twenty-seven years clerk to the parish; he worked for Mr. Woodhouse. The largesse of Mr. Knightley can surely be counted on here!"

"Mrs. Knightley, please give my most sincere regards to your husband," said Mr. Perry, who appeared as genuinely offended by Mr. Churchill's intrusion into the matter as did Emma. "You tell me old Mrs. Bates has suffered a breakage of her spectacles. As I call on her now in any case, you may rest easy in the knowledge that I shall take them with me to the young lady who works in my dispensary: she is remarkably nimble with her fingers!"

"But I insist, my dear Mrs. Knightley!" said Frank, stepping forward as if he had seen nothing of the effect caused by his most recent piece of impertinence. "I have mended old Mrs. Bates's spectacles before. Pray permit me to do so again." And so saying – without, as Emma noted with a glow of indignation, a thought for the un-suitability of his visit to the aunt of the young woman whose life and prospects he had so unthinkingly ruined – Frank Churchill stepped into the house that was but a few steps down the street from them, and mounted the stairs.

Without waiting – for she was left alone in the company of Captain Brocklehurst, Mr. Perry having scuttled after Frank, to prevent his causing too unpleasant a jolt to Miss Bates and her mother – Emma mounted into her chaise, took the reins and departed for home.

She did not look back, as the length of the street was gone down; Harriet Martin came out of Ford's, a bolt of cloth in her hand, and she received a wave and a greeting, no more. Emma was anxious to return to the Abbey; she wished for the clarity of vision of Mr. Knightley, after undergoing the slick charm of Frank Churchill; but she could not help reflecting, as she went, that Captain Brocklehurst was quite the handsomest man she had ever seen.

8

*I*t is often to be observed in those whose nature and circumstances produce a character accustomed to control and oversee the lives of others, that the unexpected is less easy to digest and understand than it is for those who have the habit of acquiescence and obedience to the demands of others. A scenario, whether domestic or abroad, which appears quite different from the one foreseen, may cause discomfiture, even rage: and it is probable that the closer to home the surprise turns out to be, the greater the need to restore order on the part of the incumbent dictator of the daily round.

So Emma, who had reflected to her own satisfaction, all the way back from Highbury to Donwell Abbey, that she had done right in choosing the company of Jane Fairfax at her dinner over that of Captain Brocklehurst (for it really was as simple as that), received an unpleasant jolt on turning into the Abbey gates and going up the drive at a complacent trot. She had known that Mr. Knightley would praise her for extending an invitation to Miss Bates and her mother, whether the niece could come or no: even that the presence of Jane Fairfax was likely to be insisted on, as a consequence of this selfless conduct on her part. Emma, though she resented Mr. Knightley's having still the ability to reduce her to tears with his censure, forgot this each time she anticipated the glow of his praise. Today, however, matters were to unfurl themselves in quite another fashion.

On the sweep before the doors of Donwell Abbey stood two people. By their stance, which was markedly not one of friendship – it could, even, as Emma discerned as she alighted from the chaise, be seen as hostile – it was easily concluded that either or both would rather be anywhere in the world than in this particular spot. Their backs were as nearly turned to each other as it was possible to be without exciting the alarm of a passing servant or arriving guest.

Across the sweep, and dabbling delightedly with their toes in a small pool, administered by a fountain and filled with water lilies, were three girls of about eight to twelve years old. Their cries of innocent happiness contrasted strongly with the sullen resentment expressed by the silent figures by the doors to the Abbey.

As Emma stood for a moment aghast – for was not this couple, of all possible conjunctions the least anticipated, here – John Knightley and Jane Fairfax, no less – a delightful laugh, not familiar to her in any way, sounded from the lime walk on the far side of the garden. From under the canopy of the trees came Mr. Knightley; and accompanying him – taking his arm, letting it loose and taking it again, none of which the squire of Donwell seemed at all to show objection to – walked a young woman in sprigged muslin, her hair piled up on her head, and with a stray ringlet or two escaping, in the very latest French mode; and with this costly arrangement of chignon and fringe Emma was indeed familiar.

As the new and unforeseen combination of persons strolled towards her, James appeared on the sweep in order to lead the horse away to the stables. Emma stood exposed before the two pairs, unknown quantities as indeed they were. She had the unpleasant sensation of having perhaps died and returned as a phantom, to find another life altogether in progress in her home; or at the very least she felt she had been gone longer and further than a brief visit to Miss Bates in Highbury. The tale of the gratitude of the two worthy ladies at a hindquarter of pork vanished from her lips; mistress of Donwell Abbey she might be, but she was rendered as silent as the pair by the Abbey doors at so great a surprise on her return. For the first time in her life, whether as Emma Woodhouse or Mrs. Knightley, she could think of nothing whatever to say.

Mr. Knightley's growing proximity returned everything to the habitual: he was not taken aback, as he appeared to take pleasure in demonstrating, by the couple who stood, as those wooden figures in a weather vane are prone to do in the English climate, half in and half out of the ancient Abbey; disengaging himself from the young beauty on his arm, he approached his wife, and, with a sardonic smile, gave a bow.

"My dear Emma, you appear flustered. It was too hot to undertake a drive to the village, I fear. My anxiety over the leg of pork you carried to the Bates household made me selfish indeed! I should not have asked it of you, to go there today."

That Mr. Knightley felt no awkwardness in mentioning the simple village custom of giving food to a poor neighbour, in front of a young lady as elegant as his companion, astonished Emma; but she admired him for his aplomb, all the same. This thought was succeeded one minute later by the reflection that Mr. Knightley's position as squire of Donwell Abbey gave him all the latitude he needed: again for the first time, Emma saw herself not as mistress of a fine house, as she had been at Hartfield, but as a mere appendage of Mr. Knightley, with neither money nor possessions of her own. She wished she had not given over Hartfield as a school for her nephews and nieces, and had retained it for her own use when she felt the need to be alone. All this passed before her eyes in a flash; and she had no sooner evacuated the premises in her mind than a strong sense of shame caused her to fill it again, this time to include the three charming little girls by the fountain, who ran up to join the party.

Introductions had to be made, at this point; and Mr. Knightley effected them. Still with an air of secret delight, he brought it to Emma's attention that she had long waited to meet Jane Fairfax again, since that young lady had last been in the county.

"And may I present, dear Mrs. Knightley, the Baroness d'Almane," said Jane Fairfax, stepping forward. The speechlessness which appeared to have descended on the couple Emma had hoped would meet, fall in love and marry, had been dispelled by John Knightley's abrupt departure down a side path in the direction of the vegetable gardens. It was evident to all that he was in a very ill humour indeed; and that one minute more in the company of the lovely governess intended for him in the heart of his sister-in-law would have proved a full sixty seconds too many.

The Baroness d'Almane was, however, too much of a diversion for thoughts of John Knightley to last any longer than that aforementioned stretch of time. She was so pretty – her dark eyes at least as intense and certainly as lovely as those of Jane Fairfax. And she was French! Clearly of a very distinguished family! Emma, who had fallen once before for the soft blue eyes of a Miss Harriet Smith, found she could not desist from gazing into the shining, dark orbs of the Baroness. A sense that she would never succeed in ordering the Frenchwoman to do her bidding came as another unexpected feeling to add to the assortment of surprises found on her return to Donwell Abbey. This *frisson* – and here perhaps lay the greatest surprise of all – was not as disagreeable to Emma as she might have supposed.

"We are staying at the Vicarage," Jane Fairfax explained. She had seen, it might be thought by any who had observed the scene, that Mr. and Mrs. Knightley both were taken with the mysterious visitor: indeed they could not remove their gaze from her at all. But, John Knightley having left them, there was no one to remark on the effect of the Baroness on Mr. and Mrs. Knightley, except for Jane Fairfax herself; and she made much of introducing her charges, Mrs. Smallridge's three daughters, to fill the next silence – this time a silence caused by rapt admiration rather than annoyance and hostility, as the meeting earlier by the doors to the Abbey clearly had been.

As they stood – and Mr. Knightley, still enjoying himself greatly, it appeared, was the first to bring a subject to the fore, though it was merely to enquire of Miss Fairfax if she intended to go on further walking expeditions with the children and that a new bridle path from the Vicarage to the Abbey had been cut through the fields, should she and her companion choose to visit the Abbey again – a tentative figure appeared at the end of the lime walk, and after an encouraging wave from Emma, ran up lightly to join her friend.

Emma felt on firmer ground, now that Harriet Martin was by her side. The disdain she had once voiced for the simple farmer whom Harriet had married was long dispersed by Mr. Knightley's insistence on the good qualities of the young man; and besides, it looked better for Emma, now she was outshone by the French Baroness, to have an acolyte of her own. Despite Harriet's prettiness, Emma would always appear in a superior light.

"We must arrange a day for you to dine at the Abbey, Miss Fairfax," said Mr. Knightley; and his eyes lit up irresistibly at his wife's face when she heard this casual extending of an invitation she had so long begged him to extend to the poor governess. "Doubtless Emma will have asked your aunt and her mother to join us here.

John – my brother John Knightley – I believe you met in the course of walking here. He will be happy to renew the acquaintance, I am sure!"

At this Jane Fairfax stiffened. Emma bit her lip, wondering at Mr. Knightley's effrontery. For there could be little hope now of a friendship, leave alone a match, between the two of them.

Mr. Knightley could not be prevented, however, from continuing in his most cordial manner. With a look of renewed admiration, he asked the Baroness d'Almane if she would be good enough to honour his wife and himself with her company. A day was proposed, and both young ladies agreed to consult their books; and, in the case of Miss Fairfax, her employer Mrs. Smallridge.

"What a pity you cannot ask the others," whispered Harriet Martin, as the party went its separate ways, with promises to confirm the day of the great dinner party. "I mean—" as Emma looked at her enquiringly, "Mr. Frank Churchill and that handsome friend of his I saw you conversing with in Highbury, Mrs. Knightley! 'Tis a pity indeed!"

Emma, seeing Mr. Knightley go off still with a smile of triumph on his face in the direction taken by his brother, did not know which of the Mr. Knightleys she most disliked today. The one she was married to, came the answer; she turned instead to chide Harriet, for her impertinence, but the young Mrs. Robert Martin stood dreaming still on the sweep by the doors to Donwell Abbey. It was not possible to invite Captain Brockle-hurst: Harriet knew it was not.

"No – of course, Mrs. Knightley. But just think! Two beautiful strangers have come to our little part of the country in one day – is that not remarkable? Two beautiful visitors to Highbury!"

Part Two

9

*E*mma and Harriet had been walking together one morning, and, in Emma's opinion, had been talking enough of the new arrivals to their part of the country for that day. Nothing further was known of Mrs. Weston's guest, Mr. Churchill's recently-acquired brother-in-law; and no more had been seen of the young ladies ensconced at the Vicarage, along with Mrs. Smallridge and her children. The subject – which it had taken some industry on the part of Emma to banish – seemed to have gone for good, when it burst out again at the mention of the book Emma carried: for she walked to Hartfield with the dual purpose of presenting Miss Whynne with a volume suitable for the improvement of her nephews and nieces; and she brought also her crayon, that she might sit in her old garden and sketch a view long dear to her as a child.

"*Practical Education?*" cried Harriet, on hearing Emma hold forth on the subject of Maria Edgeworth's treatise— "Yes indeed, Mrs. Knightley, as always you are right to introduce new ideas to the young, indeed you are! I am only pleased that the children will learn some French now—" and here, looking slyly at Emma, she could not refrain from adding, "I do believe it is suggested that the beautiful young French lady – the Baroness – shall go to Hartfield twice in the week and tutor Mr. John Knightley's children in French. A very excellent idea, says Mrs. Elton – she said it to me yesterday, you know, for sometimes—" and here Harriet blushed as if four years of matrimony did not separate her from the first object of her love, "sometimes I walk along Vicarage Lane, especially on a fine summer's day such as we are blessed with at this time of year, to remind myself of our walks there, dear Mrs. Knightley. And I think of the time you stopped to try and mend your broken lace – oh dear!"

Emma was too annoyed on several counts to reply to this. For all that the walk to Hartfield was nearly achieved, and her father's own bluebell woods traversed, she could not feel the calm and happiness the view of her old house, with the roofs of Highbury in a tranquil vista spreading out behind it, habitually produced. The mention of the Frenchwoman coming uninvited to the school, was irksome to her: *who* had suggested it, and for what purpose, other than to undermine the position of the aunt as custodian of the young Knightley family, was not difficult for her to guess. Mrs. Elton's hand was visible in all this. The second cause of Emma's annoyance lay in the fact that Harriet was too dim to understand the veiled mark of disrespect to the mistress of Donwell Abbey. "The children will do better with a good grounding in education than with a heap of subjects thrown at them all at once," was all she would say. And then, as Harriet trotted beside her, looking up anxiously at the sign of displeasure in her idol's voice: "Surely the Baroness may teach French to Mrs. Smallridge's children, if she finds herself in need of refreshing her memory of her mother tongue."

Harriet agreed rapidly and nervously; and the friends walked on in silence.

"Mrs. Smallridge had hoped you would permit her children to join your school for the summer," Harriet could not desist from saying, as the gardens of Hartfield opened from woodland; and the shrubberies, as meticulously cared for as in the day of Mr. Woodhouse, offered their long or short alternatives for approaching the house itself.

Emma had selected her spot – it was to be on the longer walk, which her father had invariably traversed in summer, when the likelihood of rain or strong winds was at its most reduced – and as a stout bench, fashioned by young Abdy for the express purpose of affording repose to Mr. Woodhouse on the longer walk, stood waiting for her, Emma sat down upon it and pulled her sketching book from her bag. Harriet, as disconcerted by the reception of her innocent remarks as Emma was made irascible by them, gave a little cry of pleasure.

"Oh, what a perfect spot to choose, Mrs. Knightley! Why, you have the countryside and the village together, at your feet. And the plants and bushes all in front – it is most picturesque!"

As the young farmer's wife spoke the wind increased a little, and a burst of childish voices floated from the walls of Hartfield. Emma, putting her head to one side, frowned. "I hear something strange, Harriet. Is it a jest my nephews and nieces play, on poor Miss Whynne? Do you hear also? We are not accustomed to this sound, here."

The wind, having got up, redoubled its strength; and both Emma and Harriet were forced to hold down their hats; while, this time unmistakably, the refrains of a piano sounded even at the furthest limit of the shrubbery, and along with it a good number of youthful voices, singing in unison.

"Why, it is the *'pont d'Avignon'*," cried Harriet. "I am

so very partial to that song, Mrs. Knightley. It does make me wish Mr. Martin would want to travel abroad – like Mr. Knightley once did—"

Emma frowned; and had her poor little friend dared, she would have said she scowled. References to Mr. Knightley's aptitude for travel as a young man were, it seemed, as unwelcome as the proposition that the Baroness d'Almane visit Emma's school. Not for the first time since the occasion of their marriages four years ago, Harriet reflected that there was a quality she might call static, had the idea or the term been known to her, in Emma and in her union with Mr. Knightley. Why did she not wish to gallivant somewhere abroad with her husband – they had not even taken a wedding journey of any adventurous nature, having waited until it was possible to leave Mr. Woodhouse for but a fortnight's absence, and then for a tour of the seaside! Even this short journey became impossible, when Mr. Wood-house's chicken house was broken into and several of his fowls taken. Mr Knightley and his bride were needed at home. There was no change to be noted at the Abbey, either: Emma had gone from a house unaltered since the death of her mother, to the permanence of Donwell Abbey. Harriet wondered if she knew she was in a different phase of life, now, to the one she had enjoyed as Miss Woodhouse of Hartfield. Mr. Knightley was no more – and no less – than a father to her, in reality.

Such were Harriet's thoughts and musings, though her fear and admiration for her friend would not have permitted her to sum them up thus. Perfection was Mrs. Knightley of Donwell: it was only on occasions such as this one that a glimmer of suspicion entered the young countrywoman's mind, the suspicion being that Emma was altogether too rigorous in the application of her moral and practical code; and should enjoy herself sometimes, with the sense of mischief she so frequently demonstrated in the days before marriage to Mr. Knightley.

As for Emma, she seemed to think of the music and singing from her old home as almost a sacrilege; and it was only after Harriet Martin cajoled her, that she resolved to stay where she was, despite the wind and its irresistible message from France. "You are so very accomplished, dear Mrs. Knightley – you have brought your crayons all the way here and everyone awaits your delightful sketch . . . Why, since you last sat here, the copper beech is down in the storm and there is an entirely new prospect, across the village. We all await your rendering of it, Mrs. Knightley!"

Harriet cried out that the wind brought the hour, in the chimes of the church clock by the Vicarage – that it was grown far later than she had dreamed it to be – that dear Robert awaited her, and she had promised him a shepherd's pie for his midday meal.

"I must fly, Mrs. Knightley. You will promise to show me your delightful sketch when it is done? Oh, look who comes! What a strange coincidence: were we not talking of him this morning as we walked here, though I believe we spoke of Jane Fairfax's French companion more. They say she was abducted, you know – I wished to inform you—"

Emma looked out across the shrubbery, her sensation being that of the listener to tales of imagined beings – Odysseus, maybe, or the hunter Actaeon on his pursuit of the fair Diana – who then sees that mythical being appear in the landscape before him. Her crayon was poised. The background to the picture became of a sudden a great deal more interesting than before; and as the foreground of the anticipated sketch now grew in appeal with the approach of the figure on horseback, she felt all the unexpectedness of gratitude, that she had not gone down to Hartfield to complain of the noise.

A Frenchwoman might be in there, for all she cared, instilling in her nephews and nieces songs they had no ability to understand.

But here, and now drawing level with her as Harriet made off as fast as she could through the beech wood to Donwell, was none other than Captain Brocklehurst, astride a very fine chestnut mare. Mr. Frank Churchill was not with him, was Emma's last conscious thought.

Captain Brocklehurst, dismounting, bowed with a

most particular smile to Mrs. Knightley, and asked if he might witness the sketch of a draughtswoman of whom everyone in Highbury spoke with unstinting praise.

"You do me too much honour, sir," said Emma; but her eyes danced and her colour – as Harriet would have noted, had she turned in her headlong flight to domestic harmony – turned a most becoming shade of pink.

10

*H*uman nature is so well inclined to the receiving of compliments, that any amount of annoyance or interference will go unchecked, in order for the succession of pleasant remarks to continue.

So it was, on the rustic bench at Hartfield that day. Songs – and on occasion lively airs played on the pianoforte – emanated with increasing frequency from the open windows of the house. Cheers, of a suspiciously rabble-rousing nature, rose at intervals. Despite all this, Emma could be perceived to be sitting as still as a statue; or, as indeed was the case, as model for the artist's pen: for, while Captain Brocklehurst spoke, he drew; and the expertise and fluency with which he wielded the crayon, taken slyly from her box, served only as further proof of the extent of connoisseurship of the young man.

"This is an unexpected honour," the Captain had said, "to find the subject – the most beautiful in Surrey – and to find the means by which I may make an attempt, however humble, to depict her—"

"You must not leave out Box Hill," said Emma, laughing. "Another famous landmark, Captain. You must not neglect to visit there and to paint – if you are regular with the brush, as I suspect."

"Indeed, I am; but Box Hill does not have heavenly eyes," came the reply, with perhaps too practised an ease. "Nor, if I may say so, the distinguished line of neck and head. Ah yes, Mrs. Elton has told us of her husband's travelling to London – before they were married, naturally! – solely in order to have a likeness of you framed, Mrs. Knightley. Is that not the case?"

"No, it is not," said Emma, who found that laughter was putting her in a better frame of mind than she had known since the disastrous day of John Knightley's accidental meeting with Miss Fairfax – and his subsequent ill humour, which continued to affect her own. "The sketch Mr. Elton took to London was *by* me, I fear; *I* was not the subject. That was Harriet Smith – Mrs. Martin, as she is now."

"But Mr. Elton took the trouble to go all the way to

the capital for the fair talents of an exceptional person," put in Captain Brocklehurst, eagerly. "If the portrait he carried showed the head of a Miss Smith, it was of the head of a Miss Woodhouse that he dreamed when he undertook the mission."

Emma could not help smiling at the dexterity of her portraitist's extrication from his *gaffe*: she wondered, however, why he had come to be on intimate terms with Mrs. Elton, and how.

"If you will be good enough to turn a little in the direction of the orchard, Mrs. Knightley. Ah yes, it is most affecting. It is sad indeed that Mr. Woodhouse, of whom I have heard so much, cannot be here to see his daughter drawn, rather than always drawing: complimented instead of constantly working for the benefit of others, however ungrateful they might be!"

Emma found her complacency brought to an abrupt halt by this tone of familiarity. Frank Churchill must be the one who confided stories of the past, to his brother-in-law: Emma knew him as indiscreet, and paused, thinking back on those matters, not secret but not in need of an airing, either, which had constituted her past life at Hartfield.

"Do not be concerned, please, Mrs. Knightley – I have brought a frown to your lovely face and I must wait until it is gone before I continue to draw it," cried the Captain, laying down the crayon. "Be assured that instinct guides me, not tittle-tattle: I saw you by the door of a simple house in the street at Highbury – at Miss Bates's. There, I have said it. I saw your degree of concern for others, your desire that lives not blessed as yours has been should not founder on the rocks of poverty or misfortune."

"Indeed it is so," said Emma sighing; and she could not help herself from reflecting that Captain Brocklehurst was very handsome – more handsome, by far, than Mr. Churchill, there was no denying it. That he was more sensible also to the efforts made by Emma to assist those with fewer advantages than herself only caused an increase in the good looks of the new visitor to Randalls. It was a pity, a very great pity, came the next thought, that Captain Brocklehurst could not be invited to the dinner at Donwell Abbey – an occasion in which Emma had lost all interest, since the evident mutual dislike of John Knightley and Miss Fairfax. The whole party was a grave mistake. If Mr. Knightley had permitted it, she would have found a reason to cancel the evening altogether.

"The frown of the goddess does not diminish," said the Captain softly. "There are too many responsibilities, on such slender shoulders. Shall we walk in the beech woods? Now your companion has fled, may I accompany you to the Abbey?"

Emma shook her head, but rose nevertheless and

made her way down the winding path in the shrubbery towards the house. As she went, a teasing, happy, rebellious jig burst out of the drawing-room windows; and she halted. The Captain soon caught up with her. "Those will be the melodies Miss Fairfax's friend has brought with her. She was in exile in Switzerland – so she informed Mrs. Elton. A very dramatic life indeed, so I understand – and still so young!"

Emma, who often reflected that her life lacked drama in the extreme, stopped again, and turned to look up at the Captain, giving him a demure glance.

"But the style of her life . . . her adventures in wild lands . . . has told on her," said Captain Brocklehurst in a grave tone. "She has not the freshness – the incomparable loveliness—" He broke off; it was too evident he referred to Emma. Blushing at her determination to extract a further compliment from him, she walked on.

"Let me say, dear Mrs. Knightley, that Frank is devastated by the fate of Miss Fairfax."

Emma felt, for a moment, the brush of the Captain's fingers against her hand: to disguise her knowledge of it, she pulled a head of lavender from the low hedge by the path and lifted it to her nostrils. She had not wished to speak of the scandal of Highbury – as it remained, even after four years. But she had a strong sense at that moment that there would be a scandal this summer, which would make the jilt of Miss Fairfax by Frank

Churchill a small misdemeanour of the past. What this would be, she could not say; but, standing now by the tall yew at the side of Hartfield, and with a waltz floating out from the windows beyond, her sense was that here and now was the beginning of the imbroglio: it was to do with the music, and the strong scent of lavender, and the sudden feeling that freedom lay somewhere in the future, even if she had not known how to embrace it in the past.

"My sister was as good as ordered by our father to marry Frank," continued the Captain. "I have a duty to tell you this, Mrs. Knightley, for you have Miss Fairfax's interests at heart, I know. It must be hard indeed for the poor girl to have us come here to Randalls. But it was so long since Mr. Weston had seen his son. It was not known that Mrs. Smallridge would invite herself for the summer to the Vicarage. When Mrs. Weston wrote to Frank of it, he asked me to come south with him, as an aid in an uncomfortable situation. I was happy to assist him.— If I do, which I doubt," added the charming young man in tones of great modesty. "We can travel about together, you know, Mrs. Knightley – it is less likely that Frank will come face to face with Miss Fairfax. That would be dreadful indeed."

"Dreadful," echoed Emma, who had in her mind placed Captain Brocklehurst at her table at Donwell Abbey and made Jane Fairfax and Frank Churchill so little interested in each other that their contiguity was of no importance at all. Now, of course, she saw this as impossible.

"Frank still loves her," said Captain Brocklehurst in a low voice behind Emma. "It is as hard for him, as it is for Miss Fairfax. And there is no greater pain," continued the gallant Captain, as the music in the house abruptly stopped and a medley of children's voices called out, as a new game was embarked on, "no more excruciating agony, than to love from afar: to worship and yet not to speak of it. Do not you agree, Mrs. Knightley?"

11

*G*reat was Emma's consternation when once she had left the environs of Hartfield and run – or walked so rapidly there was no distinguishing it from a full-fledged run – through the beech woods which separated her old home from her new one: new, as still she found it, though there were those recently come to Highbury who had not known a Miss Woodhouse of Hartfield: Mrs. Knightley, staid and well settled at the Abbey, was all they had ever heard.

She was not staid on this occasion. Captain Brocklehurst had been too forward.— Yet each time she upbraided him in her mind, his handsome face obtruded, and she smiled, as she hurried along a path she took with Harriet, or sometimes with Mrs. Weston, but seldom alone.— He had suggested he accompany her.— No, certainly not! Emma must return to Donwell Abbey without an escort; but she wished from the bottom of her heart that she had not permitted little Mrs. Martin to dash off like that and leave her to her thoughts along the way. He was the handsomest man, certainly, ever to visit Highbury.

There were few pleasant memories, for Emma, of the last quarter of an hour at Hartfield before her abrupt departure. Miss Whynne had stepped out of the French windows to the drawing-room, and had come to the corner of the shrubbery; she had seemed unsurprised to see Mrs. Knightley there, and had paid no attention to Captain Brocklehurst at all. She was so very sorry – one thing had led to another.— The Baroness had brought the Smallridge children— And now here they were, running out to play hunt-the-slipper in the bushes, as Emma would never have permitted in her days as her father's châtelaine. She did hope Mrs. Knightley would understand. As for the music – were they not the liveliest tunes? The Baroness had brought them from France – all committed to memory, dear Mrs. Knightley; not a note written down. Is not it most extraordinary?

Had Emma looked back truthfully over the preceding exchange, she might have reproached herself for being cold and distant to the poor governess. Was it not the case that Emma pitied governesses?— that she did all she could . . . though to no avail, and here she felt a lack of gratitude on the part of Miss Fairfax that she had not at least shown her thanks to her benefactress for imagining a match between herself and John Knightley, even if she knew nothing of it, and there had been a mutual dislike that was quite remarkable. But she did not think of Miss Fairfax.—

For Emma it was not difficult to steer her thoughts elsewhere. She must remember Miss Whynne; and the rebuke she had administered outside the drawing-room windows at Hartfield had gone quite beyond what was necessary, she knew. "Oh, Mrs. Knightley, I quite understand! Of course there was no arrangement that there should be music lessons here! Yes, I shall accompany the Smallridge children immediately to the Vicarage. I know their mother will be most profuse in her apologies, Mrs. Knightley!"

Throughout all this, Captain Brocklehurst stood very still and looking as fine as a statue, by the tallest shrubs; and Emma fancied he concealed a smile: this enraged and embarrassed her even further to remember, though it was true that Miss Whynne, before relapsing into servility, had shown an almost revolutionary spirit. Emma thought he frowned at the loudness of her voice and gaiety of expression. The Baroness might bring equality and liberty where she pleased, concluded

Emma, as she slowed her pace, the familiar stone walls of Donwell coming into view; but she should not infect the servants here. Miss Whynne was not a servant. Thus replied Emma's sense of fairness, and she paused, dropping almost to a saunter, as she examined her treatment of poor Miss Whynne. Then she picked up again; and walked to the gardens, where late roses appeared to greet her with an accordance of her views, each white bloom bending on a fragile stem: Miss Whynne was in the employ of Emma's brother-in-law; and doubly so, of Mr. Knightley's brother; and it would be unacceptable in the extreme if the governess were to inculcate her charges with Revolutionary songs. And neglect the mathematics!— It was with some embarrassment that Emma at this juncture realised she had brought back with her the book she had intended to leave at Hartfield, *Practical Education*.

A man approached the doors of Donwell, and he stood awhile, as if expecting to be met there, twisting his cap in his hands as he waited.

Emma recognised young Abdy, an ostler at the Crown Inn; she recalled hearing his father, who had long suffered from rheumatic gout, was on his deathbed, and, as so often before, she admonished herself for failing to visit the old man regularly.— Now it was too late. Something told her young Abdy brought bad news. He had received relief from the parish council, had he not?

But Emma knew, with a sinking of the heart, that Mr. Knightley had refused to aid the family directly, and had referred Abdy to the parish, even as his father lay dying. She knew also that there were those who considered Mr. Knightley to lack generosity in the matter.— Mrs. Weston, loved by Emma, was amongst them; and she, who in turn loved Emma, would not give away her ideas on the subject for the world.

However, there was no mistaking them.

All this had at least the effect of banishing Captain Brocklehurst's face, with its bright blue eyes and silky dark moustache, from Emma's thoughts. She paused, as if the very object of being out of doors on this day in late summer had been to pick roses for the house; and she snipped a bloom betwixt finger and thumb; not without pricking herself on a thorn. She stood a moment without any feeling of dismay, as the blood trickled from her finger. The wide doors swung open, and Mr. Knightley stepped out. Still twisting his cap, young Abdy went up close to him. Both set off down the lime walk.

Emma did not at first suffer any emotion other than slight surprise. Surely Mr. Knightley had seen her there? Was it not a demonstration of a lack of cordiality quite outstanding even in one as taciturn and reserved as Mr. Knightley, not to greet his own wife on her appearance at home after an expedition such as she had undergone?

But then, how could Mr. Knightley know what Emma had undergone? And how could she describe it, in any case? She blushed, when she thought of all the unbidden feelings which had come to visit her, in the brief hour since she was last at the Abbey: she had had no chance *other* than thinking of them, but nevertheless, there they were: she had listened to Captain Brocklehurst; she had upbraided poor Miss Whynne in no uncertain manner; she had denied access to her school to the very children she had secretly planned to include there, if her pedagogic plans prospered.

Yet Mr. Knightley had no idea at what hour she had left the Abbey and walked to Hartfield; she had to admit it would be childish indeed to upbraid him for not knowing her gone. She might have been gone ten minutes, or five; she could have turned back, suspecting rain.

It was with a sense of determination which lifted the spirits that Emma resumed her progress towards the house. She did not like the fact that her husband was so reserved – even disgustingly so; for she could, after all, have been gone hours for all he knew; but she had decided that she would not be deterred by this repulsive quality in anyone, whether married to them or no.

Jane Fairfax who was of this same reserved temperament – it was a great deal harder to make a match for her than Emma had hoped – must meet and fall in love with Captain Brocklehurst. It was this which sustained Emma through the remainder of a trying day.

12

*D*ear Emma, I do believe the little matter of our entertaining several people here to-morrow evening is no longer of any concern to you. Can you recall, even, who they are? I confess I need to scrutinise the list again, myself: we decided against Mr. and Mrs. Cole, did we not, on the grounds that they would very likely ask us back, and we could not tolerate an evening in their company, is that not so?"

Mr. Knightley spoke; and, as he did so, as Emma well knew, he teased her. They were in the library; Mr. Knightley sat at his desk, with paper and blotter laid out, as if to adjudicate on the sins of entertaining. Emma stood by the window, aware, in a reflection cast on the glass, of her slim figure in a white dress, and of a face which could appeal to some, if not to Mr. Knightley. She disliked his teasing extravagantly.

"My belief is that you are prejudiced against asking anyone to the Abbey," said Emma. "You were used to dine out as a bachelor; or to come to Hartfield, for a meal; and it does not strike you as necessary to invite people to the Abbey, and go to the trouble that involves."

"Prejudiced? I am not prejudiced. I dream night and day of the pleasures of tomorrow evening. And brother John likewise. He has told me so himself."

Emma flushed. She could not bring herself to think of a seating plan at her table which would divide John Knightley sufficiently from Jane Fairfax. Safety in numbers were needed: she knew Mr. Knightley well enough to suspect he would say as much when next he spoke.

"We are too few," said Mr. Knightley, confirming this suspicion. "Should we not invite Mr. and Mrs. Elton, late though it may be in the day? They are owed an invitation – but you are the mistress of Donwell Abbey, dearest Emma. It is not for me to judge."

Emma had thought exactly the same, but she did not care to own it. The dreadful lack of Mrs. Weston and her party threw them up against the Eltons. There was no escaping it.

The noise Mrs. Elton makes will disguise the silence between the very people whom I had wished to meet and commune in a delight of mutual discovery, thought Emma.

"Yes, I will invite Mr. and Mrs. Elton," she replied, though in a tone that was far from gracious. "But we shall be obliged to ask Mrs. Smallridge also – and when we do, that will leave Jane Fairfax's French friend alone at the Vicarage. We would be considered inhospitable in the extreme."

Emma could not confess her lack of desire to see the young woman who had had the audacity to drop in on Hartfield this morning and teach songs and airs to her nephews and nieces. She thought of telling Mr. Knightley about this, but remained silent. All her thoughts were now on a future occasion, when Captain Brocklehurst and Jane Fairfax might see each other and fall in love. She had already determined on fixing a day for the boating party, to be held on the mysterious lake recently included in the Donwell demesne. An outdoor occasion would do best, for the encounter – then Frank Churchill, if he were one of the party, could wander off and thus avoid an embarrassing reunion.

"Emma, you are dreaming again," Mr. Knightley said. "I have just remarked that I have no objection whatsoever to entertaining the Baroness d'Almane. A charming young lady! And our nephews and nieces would benefit greatly from speaking French with her, I am sure!"

Emma, who did not like Mr. Knightley's appreciation of the Baroness any more than she had savoured the handsome Captain's description of that person's wild and adventurous past, remained by the window, without a word to give in reply.

"So that is arranged, then," said Mr. Knightley, closing his blotter. "There is another matter of which I should apprise you, Emma."

At this swift assumption of domestic convenience, Emma sprang forward, her reticence forgotten. "It is not so easy to arrange as you imagine, dear Mr. Knightley! Mr. and Mrs. Elton; Mrs. Smallridge; the Baroness: five heads more, when we have already Jane Fairfax, Miss Bates and her mother; and—"

Here, to her annoyance, Emma suffered a lapse in memory. There was another guest, whom she did not mention; but no name came to her lips.

"You forget John Knightley."

Emma frowned. But a point had been gained: she was to be teased again, and there was no getting away from it.

"He was the reason, was he not, for your desire to entertain in the first place?" said Mr. Knightley, smiling. "You expressed anxiety, beloved Emma, at the solitary nature of my brother's existence. You thought he should meet a young lady – nay, I will name her – Miss Fairfax. You were of the opinion that John would be a happier man if he were to sit at table with Jane Fairfax. You think of her often, Emma. I am only surprised that you have not yet found the time to call on her. She and her friend walked here, after all, several days ago!"

"We shall need to take your mother's table into the dining-room," said Emma, for she had resolved not to hear Mr. Knightley's jibes on the subject of Miss Fairfax. "And Mrs. Hodges must prepare twice the number of patties. I would not like to see Mrs. Bates go short because of a sudden influx of new guests at the Abbey."

"Indeed not," said Mr. Knightley gravely. But the mention of moving his mother's table clearly had irked him: it was now his turn to rise, and walk around the room, nearly colliding with his wife as he did so.

"I said just now there is another matter . . ." he began.

"If it concerns old Abdy," said Emma.— She spoke crossly, and quickly regretted it. For death and social bickering were not a suitable conjunction. "If young Abdy came to tell you his father died, I am sorry," she added in a softer voice.

"Dear Emma, you are always so thoughtful," came the rejoinder. "But old Abdy has made a recovery, I am happy to say. No, it is a matter which I find difficult to decide upon—"

At this moment the door to the library opened and

John Knightley walked in. He smoked a pipe; he had come in from the garden; and, as was his wont, he was unaware of the smoke and strong odour of smouldering tobacco which preceded and remained with him, wherever he went. Emma walked over to open the window. The day was still and airless: she found her brother-in-law's habit intolerable at the best of times.

"What is it you say?" demanded John of Mr. Knightley. "There is some matter on which my considered opinion would be useful. Is there not?"

Emma sighed. She wondered at John Knightley's ability to come in at the most inconvenient moment, despite his apparently constant ill humour and consequent determination to be left to his own resources.

"Young Abdy was here," said Mr. Knightley. "He wishes for permission to build up the barn in the garden of their cottage. His sister comes from Bristol, victim of a disastrous marriage; with three children; they have nowhere to go."

"So they say," put in John Knightley, drawing on his pipe. "No proof is furnished of the homelessness of the former Abdy girl, I take it?"

"None," replied Mr. Knightley, looking slightly surprised.

"I'm sure young Abdy would hardly wish to fabricate the story," cried Emma. "You must give permission—" and she turned to Mr. Knightley; but she knew her voice to be shrill. The cloud of unpleasantly scented smoke about John Knightley's head accounted for it; she determined to have nothing more to do with the subject, and crossed the room, to the door.

"Emma – you put in a plea and then you leave!" exclaimed John Knightley. "We need you to give your reasons for advocating so reckless a decision on the part of the Donwell Estate. Have you an idea of the precedence which will be set, if brother George gives permission for the renovation of Abdy's barn? The entire village will be up in arms. Half of the populace will decide to add new houses to the most decrepit sheds in their gardens; the other half will object furiously to the privilege accorded to young Abdy. No, if the girl has led a life that is not blameless, then she must suffer the results of her iniquity!"

"More prejudice!" cried Emma. She knew her face had flushed to the roots of her hair. "You cannot call yourself impartial, sir. You do not know the details of the Abdy daughter's life. She is very likely married to a drunkard and a brute—"

"This she should have discovered, before tying the knot," came John Knightley's reply. "It is not for the Abbey to pay for such mistakes."

"John has right on his side," said Mr. Knightley, after Emma looked to him for an answer. "If a decision in favour of the woman and her family taking up residence in old Abdy's barn leads to an examination of morals and marriage, we are best out of the matter."

"But if she can be proved to be blameless—" cried Emma, who was by now more exercised by the fate of one she had not even been aware of, a few days earlier, than she had been in her life before by any issue. "What then, if it can be shown? Surely she can bring her family to Highbury—"

"The strongest argument against permitting the renovation of the building," said John Knightley; and here a mountainous cloud of smoke came from his pipe, investing him with an air at once ridiculous and oracular, "the conclusive argument must lie in the law."

"Ah. Yes," said Mr. Knightley, but he did not dare look at Emma.

"The statute which forbids trespass on land that is due to be enclosed," said the lawyer from within the smoke. "To contravene the law would be to bring the matter to assizes, brother George. And the case would almost certainly be lost."

"That settles it," muttered Mr. Knightley. His eyes had not followed his wife; and now he shuddered as the door to the library was shut with a loud clamour. The two brothers Knightley stood alone, facing each other in the room.

"I forget," said John, puffing. "Is the dinner party tonight, or tomorrow night? I had an idea I might go to visit the land just added to Donwell, and take Henry and John with me: Henry has said he wishes to be a surveyor when he is older; we can measure it out together and return late at night."

Mr. Knightley said the dinner was due to take place on the following day. "I am sure your absence would be much remarked on," he said in a mild tone as the two men parted and went their separate ways.

13

Emma's very good opinion of Mr. Knightley was severely shaken by the scene in which she had reluctantly participated in the library. He did not have the courage of *her* convictions; that was the beginning and end of it; but she did not wish to accept so great a gulf in their ways of thinking.

Mr. Knightley's fixture at the Abbey had been as certain as the constellations, to Emma, all her sentient life: how he had directed his farm, his sheep and his library had never once occurred to her. It had not seemed pertinent, to the way in which she esteemed – and even, as she told herself, was in love with him. Mr. Knightley was himself: the Abbey, which had stood there as long, in Emma's childhood, as its squire, was administered invisibly, and ran according to the laws of Nature rather than of man.

For this reason, her spouse's parsimony and moralising tone on the subject of his tenants had come as a rude shock. Perhaps he would speak differently to her, later, and only wished to placate the legal mind of his brother John. But he had never shown the least desire to agree with the lawyer before. No, these were Mr. Knightley's own views. And Emma thought the less of him for them.

She took a shawl and determined to walk down to old Abdy's cottage. She would see for herself: if there was one thing Emma hated, it was concealment or secrecy, and a brief interview with young Abdy's wretched sister would suffice. On the way home, she would make a detour to the Vicarage. The invitation to dinner on the morrow would bear all the charm of spontaneity, if delivered by the mistress of Donwell Abbey herself. The fact of Miss Bates's chattering about the event – but Emma did now dread how Miss Bates chattered – should not detract too much from the lateness of the call to dine with the first family of Highbury. Mrs. Elton would be only too delighted; it was true that Mr. and Mrs. Knightley had a month back suffered an al fresco repast in the Vicarage garden, which only a fierce burst of rain had prevented from going on far too long. It was time the Eltons, for all their aspirations and pretensions, were invited to dine within the Abbey walls.

Thinking of Mrs. Elton's forthcoming and undoubted pleasure at Emma's inclusion of their young French friend, not to speak of the unlimited kindness shown by the hostess in inviting Mrs. Smallridge, Emma found her thoughts straying rapidly from the indignation she had felt at Mr. Knightley's prejudice, and returning to the vexed subject of Jane Fairfax and a possible betrothal between the poor governess and the dashing Captain Brocklehurst.

Emma could not say why, but these thoughts were especially delicious to her: she could picture Miss Fairfax on the day when Highbury Church bells pealed out; she could go so far as to see the happy couple settled in Yorkshire, with Jane not worried one whit by the proximity of Frank Churchill; she saw them dine by candlelight, in a house as ancient as, but a good deal smaller than, her own. Beyond that, prudence and delicacy could not take her. But the urgency with which she contemplated her duties in the matter assured her it was fortunate she had decided to call at the Vicarage on her way back from visiting the poor. For if she went one half day more without actually speaking to Jane Fairfax, Mr. Knightley would tease her horribly at her insistence on matchmaking for people she did not even find the time to see.

The day was fine; the morning's wind had dropped and the few clouds, which had threatened to turn from white to a darker hue, now strayed away altogether. The lanes were filled with flowers, which gave off a heady scent. Emma thought she had never found Highbury's humble environs so lovely.— No wonder indeed that young Abdy's sister wished to settle here, after life in a choking city such as Bristol, where smoke from chimneys brought a haze undesirable to any person country-bred. Emma was disposed to contravene Mr. Knightley's decision and give the unhappy woman tenure of the old barn here and now. Did this not in any case free her brother for his duties at the Crown Inn? And thus relieve the parish from supporting the family, while he cared for his old father? Emma's mind was never far from being practical. The Abdy sister would nurse the old man.— Once this was fixed, Mr. Knightley was certain to approve the plan.

As she rounded the bend in the lane which would bring her to Abdy's cottage, Emma saw to her annoyance that Frank Churchill, alone this time and on foot, approached. He paused from time to time and plucked a flower from the hedge: by the time he was standing close up to her, an armful of blooms, prettily enough arranged, as Emma had to admit, were encircled by wide leaves and tied with a rustic stem.

"Mrs. Knightley! There is no one I would rather encounter on so magical a midsummer's walk as this!" And with these words came a low bow, and the bouquet was thrust into her hands.

"I thank you, Mr. Churchill. But it really is not convenient. I am on my way to visit old Mr. Abdy. Then I proceed to the Vicarage. Wild flowers wilt so easily – I think it is best you take them back to Randalls. Mrs. Weston will be well pleased with them – she much prefers Nature's offerings to hothouse blooms."

Frank Churchill, despite Emma's attempting to thrust the bunch back at him, did not extend his hands but stood instead, head to one side, and contemplating what he saw with undisguised admiration. "May I say, Mrs. Knightley, that marriage suits you exceedingly well? We have not had a chance to speak to each other – I do not count our brief glimpse by Miss Bates's house—"

Here Frank fell silent, as if to demonstrate his grief at any mention, however fleeting, of the aunt of the woman he had loved and then abandoned.

"I thank you again, Mr. Churchill. But I must depart. The sun is hot, and old Abdy will need to rest. I shall miss him altogether."

Emma found herself much annoyed by the encounter with Frank Churchill. His look of blatant appreciation only served to remind her of the flirtation she had permitted him to embark on with her, and particularly on the occasion of the picnic at Box Hill. She decided he was by no means as handsome as his brother-in-law Captain Brocklehurst.

"Mrs. Knightley, you have said you intend to call on

the Vicarage when you have performed your commendable charity – commendable indeed, in a heat such as this! May I ask of you one favour – a small favour indeed, but I do not know what else to call it—"

Emma resumed walking; she had returned the flowers to Frank with some firmness, but he was not deterred from walking close to her side in the narrow lane. The thatch of old Abdy's cottage came into sight. It was as derelict, Emma noted with a sinking heart, as it had been in winter: did not Mr. Knightley's factor consider building up a new roof for the poor old man in the fine weather, that he might find relief from his rheumatic gout when frost and rain came again? Concerned with this matter, Emma walked on in deep thought: she did not at first hear or understand Frank Churchill's request.

"Mrs. Knightley! You are known throughout Highbury for your open, generous nature. This is so little to ask of you. But the pleasure – the reassurance – it would afford—"

Emma saw the bouquet was yet again proffered. She frowned.

"Ragged robin. Campion, and speedwell. Foxgloves and wild strawberry, lords and ladies so erect and orange as they stand—"

Emma stared at her companion. It occurred to her that sudden wealth and change of circumstances could have altered Frank Churchill beyond recognition. It was certainly strange to her that he should recite the names of flowers to her. Yet there was some charm in his knowing them, she had to admit.

"To give this bouquet to Jane – to Miss Fairfax, as you are visiting the Vicarage. These – yes, dear Emma – we are old friends, please permit me – these were her favourite flowers, in summer. But spring, naturally, she loved most of all. The primrose! The violet! These come late and sparsely to Yorkshire, if at all. She will understand.— You do not speak—"

Emma, arriving at the gate to old Abdy's cottage, was too astonished at first by Frank Churchill's request to notice the condition of the wicket gate, which hung from its hinges, each spar of wood in the final stages of rot. Her reaction – what succeeded her surprise – was anger; and she did not care if he knew it. That she should be taken advantage of, as a go-between! It was monstrous; disgusting! She did not know how to reply.

The path to the cottage door was overgrown with weeds. Young Abdy, yawning and rubbing his eyes, came down it to open the gate; it was not easy to know, from his bemused expression, whether he welcomed the mistress of Donwell's visit or not, on so hot an afternoon as this.

"I am come to enquire after your father," said Emma,

and as she spoke the door to the cottage opened once more and a young woman, exceedingly white-skinned and as freckled all over as a robin's egg, came out into the glare of the sun. Emma almost immediately disliked her; but she suppressed the feeling, for she knew that appearances could be misleading: she had no wish to be as prejudiced as Mr. Knightley, and with more grounds than he for her dislike. But Abdy's sister – as she surely must be – had a face so disagreeable, and a manner of walking, as she approached, so lewd and disrespectful, that Emma found it hard to keep her eyes on her throughout the introduction effected by old Abdy's son.

Frank Churchill, at least, was put in his place by the arrival of the two younger Abdys by the gate to the cottage. Murmuring his excuses – and still holding the bouquet – which, as Emma noted with some amusement, wilted already – he walked off at a brisk pace whence he had come. Back to Randalls, as Emma supposed, for the lane would take him there in ten minutes.

Emma was asked to step indoors, where, as she also saw with some misgivings, the arrival of the daughter had done little to bring order or cleanliness to old Abdy's hovel. There was little chance the daughter's care would assuage the pain or discomfort of the old man. A hen ran in as they stood talking; and the hen was followed by two children, both boys, as speckled and ill-mannered as their mother. Scuffling broke out, and little effort was made to remove the cause of Emma's annoyance from the room.

Despite all this, she allowed herself to be led to the end of the garden, where was a barn as mouldering as the cottage itself. Representations were made, on behalf of his sister, by young Abdy.

Emma, after visiting the old man upstairs and saying she would despatch James with calf's foot jelly, took her leave of the Abdy household and continued on her way.

She could not help regretting, as she went, the impulsive manner in which she had promised young Abdy – and thus his sister – that they should use the barn and reconstruct it as they pleased.

For it occurred to her quite forcibly that Mr. Knightley might well be right, in his estimation of the dangers of encouraging a young woman so unsuitable to the gentilities of Highbury, to settle here. There had not even been a mention of a lawfully-wedded husband, father to the boys, and to a sickly-looking girl, already housed on a pile of hay in the barn.

Emma knew herself to be in the wrong. But it was a matter of principle with her, that the cottagers at Donwell should not go in want. These thoughts were, however, very soon succeeded by wonderment at the impertinence of Frank Churchill's request, and this in itself followed by further and extensive thoughts on the subject of Captain Brocklehurst. Frank might still be in love with Jane Fairfax; the difficulty lay in guiding the rightfully intended pair down the aisle of St. Mary's Church in the parish of Highbury.

14

The lawn to the Vicarage was steeply sloping, and bordered with shrubs neatly trimmed. A dovecote had been introduced, since the bachelor days of Mr. Elton – causing, as Emma, with some amusement recalled, references to the marital harmony of the parson and his wife, by that lady; not to mention additional reminders of the glory of Mrs. Elton's house of origin, Maple Grove. As well as this, a stream, which ran with some force in the most precipitous part of the garden, meandered at the base with its contingent of water-lily pads; these, as Emma was also unwillingly made to think, had been imported from that splendid mansion in the vicinity of Bristol, from a pond "twice the capacity of anything in Highbury"; and were not even to be equalled by the aquatic plantings of Mrs. Elton's friends, family and neighbours, the Sucklings and the Bragges.

Emma paused by the gate, and collected herself for the meeting with Jane Fairfax. She had dreamed and invented too long, for her own good; she must appear a casual visitor, albeit one who brought an invitation of some significance to Miss Fairfax's French friend and her employer both.— But, before she could assume the superior and pleasant air for which Mrs. Knightley was as well known as Miss Woodhouse once had been, a short, brown-haired woman appeared on the crest of the lawn; and, as if well accustomed to scampering on the turf there, came down at speed to greet the guest.

"My goodness – Oh, I do believe it is Mrs. Knightley, Augusta! Mrs. Knightley is come to call on us here!"

The announcement was answered almost as soon as it was voiced. Mrs. Elton, as tall and splendidly attired as the other was quietly clothed, descended the lawn as if obeying a summons from a deity, the only one such permitted to dictate the movements of Augusta Elton. A flat basket, filled with peonies and roses, hung on her arm. A silence accompanied the regal descent.

Mrs. Elton assured Mrs. Knightley that she and Mrs. Smallridge (for such indeed was the woman recognised by Emma as the interloper at Hartfield on the occasion of her earlier visit there) had lived in hope of a visit from Mrs. Knightley. She then proceeded to come up very close, lower her voice, and, in doing so, spill the contents of the flower basket on the ground. Mrs. Smallridge obediently stooped to pick them up.

"My dear Mrs. Knightley," said Mrs. Elton in a loud whisper, accompanied by an ejection from the lips of a spitting which was unparalleled in Emma's experience, "my dear Emma – we must speak and act with the greatest circumspection. Poor Jane—"

Here Mrs. Elton broke off, allowing Emma the opportunity of observing her companion for a possible reaction to this ominous reference to her children's governess. As Emma had imagined would be the case, Mrs. Smallridge did all she could to conceal her feelings: a clear irritation was, however, visible on her features; and, in order to conceal this further, she stooped to retrieve a fallen bloom, permitting herself a brush from a stinging nettle as she did so. The ensuing cries of compassion from Mrs. Elton; the appearance of Mr. Elton himself, at the sounds of distress from the lower area of the garden – all these assisted in a prevention of Emma's closer inspection of Mrs. Smallridge's true reactions to the subject of Miss Fairfax.

"A sting from a nettle can be very unpleasant at this time of year!" announced Mr. Elton, who bowed to Emma, handed a silk handkerchief to Mrs. Smallridge, and took his wife's hand in his all at the same time.

"There should be none of the noxious weed in the garden – I shall speak to Jesse forthwith on the subject – indeed, I shall dock his wages; he must learn, despite his young age, to do a job properly if it is to be done at all."

"Indeed, Mr. Elton, you talk of a dock," said Emma gravely. "I believe you will find that a dock leaf will bring greater relief to a nettle sting than a silk bandanna."

She walked to the side of the palisade, where further specimens of the offending weed, along with the wide-leafed medicinal plant, grew against wooden palings. Emma plucked one, and handed it to Mrs. Smallridge. The leaf was applied to the angry blister which formed on the hand; Mrs. Smallridge professed herself cured; Mrs. Elton cried out in admiration.

"We are shown to lack the countrywoman's mastery of local lore! Here, in dear Highbury, the wives and witches have not changed their ways!— No, a country herb will prove more efficacious than a surgeon, each man or woman their own apothecary! But—" and here, his wife elbowed away Mr. Elton, who appeared to have been delivered, as if by express, at the bottom of the slope only to find himself now incapable of bestirring from his pose – "but there is no potion, of modern medicine or of country history, which can cure a broken heart— do not you agree, Mrs. Knightley?"

Here, once more, Emma observed a look akin to hatred cross the face of Mrs. Smallridge. The look was directed upwards, as if the church of St. Mary placed on an eminence above the Vicarage, or at least the upper reaches of the lawn, might be held responsible for the inconvenience suffered by that personage. What did become visible, on the crest of the sward, however, was Jane Fairfax, in a white dress and carrying a bunch of flowers. Emma began to understand; and found it hard to restrain a smile.

"Poor Jane!" said Mrs. Elton once more, her whisper now modified, but loud enough to cause the young woman to whom she alluded to turn her head abruptly, in the walk she had taken to be a solitary one; and to look down, startled at the assembled group.

This is intolerable, thought Emma. A true sense of compassion filled her, for the governess who could not even walk alone without the commentary and irritation of Mrs. Elton and Mrs. Smallridge. I shall go up and rescue her. She needs to find a friend in whom she can place her confidences. She shall come back with me to the Abbey, if she so wishes; and no plea on the part of her employer shall prevent her from accompanying me.

These were Emma's thoughts, which were as rapidly succeeded by a determination to have Jane Fairfax teach at the school at Hartfield, and be freed for ever from the tyranny of the life of a governess. Yes – until she is ready to wed, went Emma's calculations. It is a better thing by far that she should be independent, before Captain

Brocklehurst brings himself to propose marriage to Miss Fairfax— And Emma imagined the beautiful young teacher at the pianoforte in the drawing-room at Hartfield, and the Captain standing by the corner of the shrubbery – just where he had stood earlier with her, entranced by the accomplishment of the young woman he would soon make his bride.

"Mrs. Knightley! My dear Emma!" said Mrs. Elton in a tone which suggested she had already attempted without success to bring herself to her visitor's attention. "I must inform you that it is all most unsatisfactory. We saw Mr. Frank Churchill – yes, none other than he – climb the wall at the eastern boundary of the Vicarage grounds, not half an hour ago. He handed a bouquet to poor Jane. She is quite undone, Mrs. Knightley!"

"The children are in the midst of their lessons," said Mrs. Smallridge. "It is hard enough to persuade the girls to read the sermons dear Mr. Elton has been kind enough to have bound for them—"

"Sermons?" cried Emma, for she saw Mr. Elton's lips swell with self-importance at the mention of his utterances from the pulpit of St. Mary's. "I think Mr. Elton is as well suited to the composing of a riddle as a sermon, Mrs. Smallridge! It is to be hoped the right album has been put before your daughters – or there will be poems and snippets recited at table that are good enough to bring a blush to any cheek!"

This reference to Mr. Elton's ridiculous riddle, presented to Emma before that reverend gentleman had had the opportunity of visiting Bath and catching there his wife, Augusta, and considered by Emma to be a manifestation of the vicar's love for Harriet Smith, brought an abrupt silence to the sunken garden. Mrs. Elton remarked on the profusion of horse flies to be found at this time of year near the river, and Mrs. Smallridge muttered that she had matters concerning her daughters to attend to, with some urgency.

"The dear Smallridge children are given a French lesson when they tire of a sermon, in the absence of Miss Fairfax," said Mrs. Elton to Emma when a measure of composure had been regained and the little party strolled along a path which followed the recently-deflected river-bed to higher ground. Emma could not help noting that the sight of the governess walking alone was thus circumvented.

"Indeed—" cried Mrs. Smallridge, who now produced a note of triumph, as if the absconding of Miss Fairfax from the schoolroom could be seen as a stroke of good fortune rather than the opposite. "Here she is! The lesson is doubtless concluded. My dear Baronne, how can I thank you for your kindness today?"

Emma, who had determined to deliver her invitation to the Eltons and their guest, for dinner at Donwell Abbey the following evening; and after this to find Miss

Fairfax and suggest to her, in the utmost confidence, that she consider a post at Hartfield when the school was permanently established there, found her speech halted at the sight of the young woman who now stepped from the open windows of the Vicarage on to the lawn. She had not seen, and for all the admiration expressed at the time, she had not understood, the extraordinary beauty and vivacity of Miss Fairfax's friend, the new visitor to Highbury.

In turn, the Baroness d'Almane walked briskly up to Emma and took her hand. Emma had only the time to see how very strong her eyebrows were – black, forceful and thick, above intense dark eyes – before Mr. Elton, betraying both awkwardness and an irritation that matched that of Mrs. Smallridge, remarked that they were all indeed most obliged to the '*chère Baronne*' for the tuition she had just delivered to the children in the Vicarage schoolroom. He murmured something to the effect that Miss Fairfax was sadly indisposed – but here came Miss Fairfax, as if summoned by his words; walking listlessly; but here nonetheless, and her hand the next to be taken by her friend.

Emma issued her invitation. Everything turned to the subject of Miss Fairfax's supposed indisposition. Mrs. Elton would send notice later. Dear Emma would be good enough to understand. Reflecting that she had succeeded once again in not encountering "poor Jane", and would therefore be horribly teased by Mr. Knightley on her return, Emma took her leave; and, refusing Mr. Elton's carriage, started on her way back to the Abbey on foot.

She would make no reference – so she determined, and would not permit anyone, least of all Mr. Knightley, to make her break her word – to Miss Fairfax's true state of mind, when she arrived home. Nor – as she would in any case be incapable of such a thing – did she have any desire to describe the unutterably altered condition of her own.

15

The day grew hotter as it wore on; and Emma would have wished she had taken the offer of Mr. Elton and his carriage if it had not been for the near certainty of the company of either the vicar or his wife, all the way to Donwell. It was preferable to walk.

Besides this, her thoughts were in turmoil. She wondered at the nature of the friendship between the Baroness and Jane Fairfax: she could not help it, but she did. Ideas of Captain Brocklehurst, the fine wedding she envisaged and the ensuing comforts of life at Enscombe – for Jane would be near Frank Churchill, she would be as a sister to him by then, as Emma had decided, and they would be lifelong friends – were all gone to dust.

What must be known; must be explained and understood, was the how, the why and the wherefore of Jane's first encounter with the Frenchwoman. What was her name? Had Jane Fairfax travelled so far – much farther than Emma herself – that she had met so fascinating a creature without, as it might be said, evincing the least surprise at such a phenomenon? Where had Jane Fairfax been?— But Emma knew Mrs. Smallridge's horizons did not stretch to Paris. Could this superior person have been met with at Weymouth? Emma's surmises went far and fast: did Colonel and Mrs. Campbell, of whom Miss Bates spoke so often, have the entrée to a world inhabited by such as the Baroness d'Almane? It seemed improbable in the extreme; but Emma cursed herself for resolutely refusing to listen in all those past years when Miss Bates had read aloud from Jane Fairfax's letters on the subject of Colonel and Mrs. Campbell, their daughter Mrs. Dixon, and the long (and to Emma insufferably trying) evenings enjoyed by that family at Weymouth.

It was not simply a question of the circles in which Miss Fairfax and the Baroness had become acquainted. There was another matter: Emma did not wish to acknowledge it to herself, but as she walked, and the heat increased, her thoughts narrowed, and dwelt only there. Jane's hand had lain a second longer than was customary, even between friends, in the Baroness's grasp. Emma recalled the cool, strong hand in which her own had been held. But only for a matter of a few trifling instants – a courtesy unnoticed by the French-woman, a greeting with no significance other than that of the most elementary politeness. Had Emma, after a first, quiet glance of appraisal, even been seen? Or seen as much or more than on the first occasion, when Mr. Knightley, much taken with the beautiful stranger to Highbury, had strolled with her in the lime walk?

No, Emma would not think of Mr. Knightley and the visitor – and if she did not, it was because a voice told her of the lack of interest in such as Mr. Knightley, in the heart of the Baroness. She cared for good company. She was exquisite. She was capable, no doubt, of inspiring admiration, even love, in the breasts of men. But the hand she held the longest would belong to Jane Fairfax, or another of her sex. Emma did not know how she was apprised of this; how she knew it, as a horse scents danger or a child the presence of love; but she did. And she knew her questions must be answered; or she would not sleep or rest.

The crest of the hill was reached, but a long trudge lay ahead before the Abbey walls were arrived at. Emma paused by the side of the road, and confessed herself to be hot, though to what extent her condition arose from the temperature of the day and how much from the novel agitation which now possessed her, it would be impossible to say. She was not sorry, therefore, to hear the wheels of a trap, as it came up the long steep hill behind her; and for a moment – but this would have been too fortunate indeed! – she thought she distinguished the sound of Mr. Perry's carriage – the very conveyance which, by meriting a mention all of four years ago in the secret correspondence of Jane Fairfax and Frank Churchill, had betrayed the existence of their clandestine engagement.

How refreshing it would be, to meet Mr. Perry here! Emma thought of the good doctor as she considered her childhood: a litany of warm and cool drinks, of wrapping up against the cold by Mrs. Weston – or "poor Miss Taylor" – to the specifications of Mr. Perry. And she recalled most of all, perhaps, the kindness of the old doctor, when her father lay dying: he had been ready to appear at any hour of the night or day. He had prescribed as great a quantity of gruel as Mr. Woodhouse could sup, and had refused him nothing that seemed to suggest itself as a remedy for the incurable ailment of extreme old age. Mr. Perry stood for all that Emma did *not* think of, at this strange time; and she welcomed the chance to have him come forward in her thoughts – wholesome, as bland and innocent as her childhood and young womanhood had been. But the carriage did not contain Mr. Perry, as soon became evident. It was Augusta Elton who drew up in her trap; the door was flung open, and Emma mounted; the day was too hot for the producing of excuses or reasons to continue with a walk.

"You departed so suddenly! My *caro sposo* and I were quite alarmed to find you flee, dear Mrs. Knightley, from our little party! But I believe you found the gathering as inconvenient as I did – is that not the case? As Mrs. Bragge always repeated to me, in the words of her aunt Lady Carinthia Bragge, it is not suitable to entertain in the company of a governess. Now your Mrs. Weston, my dear, is of course a gentlewoman, and one may say that dear Miss Bates provided a most respectable upbringing for Miss Fairfax. Nevertheless I always do find there to be trouble when a governess is concerned."

Emma flushed in annoyance. For all the speed and comfort of the little trap, she wished herself back on the hard surface of the lane again. There was one reason only, as she recognised, for accepting Mrs. Elton's offer to transport her to Donwell. She would discover the answer to those questions which preoccupied her; then, thanking the vicar's wife for her kind actions, she would climb down from the carriage and continue her journey as she had done before.

"I do not know, my dear Emma, if you are acquainted with the extraordinary life of the Baronne d'Almane," continued Mrs. Elton, thus preventing both the query and an expression of displeasure at the familiarity of address. "We have been most *bouleversés* – that is, my lord and master and myself – to hear of such adventures! – such bravery! – we are reminded of our good fortune here, in the calm of Highbury!"

Emma assured Mrs. Elton with as much discipline of her emotions as she could muster, that she had heard no word of the past life and exploits of the Baroness d'Almane. Here, as that voice told her, came the answer to the preoccupations and sorrows of Jane Fairfax – and, for Emma refused already to hear the truth as it had declared itself to her just five minutes before, here indeed was the route to the rescue of poor Jane from the miseries of her existence. Marriage must come quicker than had at first been surmised. Or Jane was lost.— Emma saw an abyss, very deep: she did not see herself fall into it. Jane must be saved from the attentions of the Frenchwoman who pursued her even here.

"Elise – her real name is Delphine – is that not a lovely name? – was born in Paris of aristocratic parents. Both were lost to the guillotine."

Emma murmured something – she knew not what. Her heart was hardened against the woman who would take Jane from the prospects of a comfortable and happy life – one such as Emma's own – and subject her to the miseries of female friendship, ostracism and despair. She did not look straight at Mrs. Elton as the

Baroness's past was exhumed; the countryside, dry and brown as the hedgerows and grass banks had now turned in the late season of the summer, was as refreshing as ever she had seen it, on the way from Donwell Abbey to Highbury.

"Delphine – Elise, I should say – was married and widowed early—"

"So young?" Emma could not help herself from exclaiming.

"Indeed, she was left a widow with a handsome portion. Such is the kindness of the Baronne's heart that she wished to aid a young girl, Mathilde, in the finding of a husband. A young man had been found for Mathilde by her mother; his name was Léonce."

The Abbey walls, still a mile or so distant, were visible at last. Emma thought she had never been so glad to see them come into view: beyond these stone-clad edifices were honour, loyalty, fidelity: all that Mr. Knightley brought to the world, as landowner and working farmer, husband and mentor. Here, as Mrs. Elton presented it, was the great world, in which acts of treachery and vile conspiracy are matters of the everyday. Never had Emma wished to run into the arms of Mr. Knightley more.

"You do not care to hear this," cried Mrs. Elton; and Emma could not refrain from observing that so great a degree of sensibility on the part of the lady of the

Vicarage was rare. "It is because you fear a tale of ill repute – you do not wish to find yourself soiled by such stories from the Continent, dear Emma!"

The trap rattled along, for the incline went gently at this point downhill to the Abbey gates. Had Emma not feared the breaking of an ankle, she would have leapt to the ground there and then; as it was, she turned a face that was by no means amiable, in the direction of Mrs. Elton. "It is not so," said Emma, though she felt a lurch within, at her own encouragement of the narrative. "Pray continue, Mrs. Elton!"

"It was the fault of no one," said Mrs. Elton, and as she raised her voice against the rattle of the small stones in the road on the wheels of the trap, she became more than customarily shrill. "Elise – Delphine, no I must allow her at this great moment in her life the honour of her own name – Delphine and Léonce fell violently in love!"

I thought as much, said Emma to herself; but she was moved, she could not say why. It had been a long, hot day: she thought briefly of Captain Brocklehurst, as women will think of the one in their secret hearts, when a love story is told – but he vanished again, before there was time, even, for him to stand in her imaginings in the Hartfield shrubbery. The Baroness – Delphine – appeared in his place: to banish this figment an effort of conscious will came into play.

"The love was known to all Paris," said Mrs. Elton.

"Delphine was disgraced. She had no choice but to wander in wild lands—"

"It was as well," said Emma, who was aware of sounding stiff.

"Until at last she came to Switzerland. There she entered a convent—"

A vision of the Baroness in nun's habit rose in Emma's mind, and was despatched with as much difficulty as the last. But Mrs. Elton talked on. The walls of the Abbey rose to greet them: the gates, closed, were opened by a lad fumbling with a key. "The mother superior was an aunt of Léonce, and it was she who brought the lovers together again. Mathilde, the last to hear of the scandal, had died in Paris, died of a broken heart—" Mrs. Elton's voice wore on; and Emma, fatigued by the tale, by the heat and by the sense of an unknown danger she had felt since leaving the Vicarage alone, begged that the conveyance be brought to a halt. It was shady in the yew drive to Donwell Abbey. She would be glad to walk.

"But one day, when Léonce and Delphine were together in the convent," continued Mrs. Elton, as she pulled in the reins and Emma descended at as great a speed as she could contrive – "one day, there came the sound of the music of a regiment beyond the walls. Léonce ran to the window. For the glory of his country he knew he must go and fight—"

Emma stood by the trap. Her head ached, and she

wished to make it clear that no answer had been given to her invitation to dinner the following day. What would Mrs. Hodges do, if she must wait until the very last minute to hear if five guests came or not? For the first time, Emma was inclined to blame Jane Fairfax: for the awkwardness over dinner; for bringing to Highbury the possessor of a lurid history which nevertheless absorbed her as no story of a life had done before; in short, for everything. She wished she had not taken Jane Fairfax's dilemma to heart. It was, after all, a very commonplace dilemma, that of a young woman who has no independence and must work for a living: how was it, then, that such thought, energy and compassion must be poured at every hour of the day into Jane Fairfax? The fact that these had not been asked for, made the question all the more infuriating.

"Léonce was killed fighting for his country," Mrs. Elton ended on a triumphant note. "Look, Emma – there is Knightley!— Why, he must have heard us coming. He has a sense when you are in the vicinity. It is most romantic, my dear!"

Emma saw that her husband did indeed approach; though the drive, with the deep shade cast by the yews, seemed from time to time to swallow him up. She walked at a brisk pace towards him; any hopes that Mrs. Elton would turn and head for home were, naturally, abandoned.

"Mrs. Knightley!" Mrs. Elton's voice came in pursuit as she came near to the man she had long known; had married; and revered and respected above all else. Already, as he smiled at the speed of her coming to him, the melodrama of the Baroness faded away. Mr. Knightley was as much England as the Frenchwoman was the other world, of which Emma knew nothing and wished to know no more. In her relief, she increased her pace further. Both husband and wife laughed as she almost threw herself into his arms.

But Mrs. Elton had drawn abreast. The pony streamed in the heat, and flies settled on its neck, so the champing and chafing of the horse almost drowned her next words. "Oh, Knightley, a very good day to you! Your dear *Signora* has had the kindness to invite us to the Abbey tomorrow. May I say we shall all be more than happy to come? With the possible exception of Miss Fairfax, I must add. She is at present severely indisposed."

Mr. Knightley, who had taken the hand extended by the Vicar's wife, expressed his hopes that Miss Fairfax would be sufficiently recovered by the following day to join them for dinner at the Abbey.

"The party is mostly in her honour, you know," he added, and had Emma not found herself to be so attached to him at that moment, she could have disliked him for the mischievous smile which accompanied these words.

"Indeed," said Mrs. Elton, "but now that an invitation has been extended to our Baronne, we shall not be short of the most delightful female company."

Mr. Knightley assured Mrs. Elton that her own presence was quite enough to make up that complement.

"I do hope," cried Mrs. Elton, for she was encouraged by admiration from a quarter previously unexpected, "that your brother John Knightley will be among the guests tomorrow, dear Mr. Knightley. For I know your esteemed wife will not be offended when I say I have long in my imagining placed the Baronne d'Almane at the side of Mr. John Knightley on this particular occasion – and now we are actually invited, I cannot resist putting the proposition discreetly to you. I trust I do not exceed my duties as hostess to a tragic noblewoman—"

But Emma, who saw Mr. Knightley unable to restrain his laughter beside her, had started her walk up the drive without turning her head to the left or the right.

It was monstrous, that Mrs. Elton should dare to try out her matchmaking at dinner at Donwell Abbey. It was insufferable, that she should place the French-woman where Emma had long in her mind placed Jane Fairfax – at the side of John Knightley. It should not be!

Captain Brocklehurst was quite forgotten, as Emma concluded her walk back to the comforts and familiarity of the Abbey. Jane Fairfax – poor Jane – must be saved from a life without hope, happiness or true harmony. She should be obliged to overcome her antipathy to John Knightley, and he must conquer his aversion to *her*.

One suspicion entertained by Emma would, however, not leave her as she walked: as soon as Mr. Knightley had persuaded Mrs. Elton to return to the Vicarage, he would come to the Abbey and tease her insufferably.

16

Emma was not required to continue thinking of her ill opinion of Mrs. Elton: that she was self-important, presuming, familiar, ignorant and ill-bred could only be repeated so many times, before a sense of impatience with the idea of the morrow's party became overwhelming; fortunately a guest – and one who was as welcome at the Abbey as Mrs. Elton would ever be the contrary – waited for her in the drawing-room. Mrs. Weston had come; and, after a conversation with Mr. Knightley on the subject of a boating party which her own incumbents at Randalls, Mr. Frank Churchill and Captain Brocklehurst, had particularly requested, she had decided to remain indoors until such time as her Emma could be seen to return safely home.

Emma was overjoyed to find her old governess there. The fears and apprehensions of the preceding hours soon vanished away. Mrs. Weston smiled at the suggestion that Jane Fairfax was truly made ill by the indignities of her profession, and said so, in words which Emma was grateful to hear.

"Beloved Emma, you care too much for the fortunes of others! Jane Fairfax is not so well placed as I was, to be sure—" and here Mrs. Weston smiled so tenderly at the memory of old Mr. Woodhouse and his wife, mother to Emma, of whom the child had remembered so little, and the grown woman almost nothing at all. "But she is well looked after at the Smallridges. She will recover from her broken heart – may I assure you, my dear, that this is possible? And then – who knows? Someone else may come into her life. And she will be happy – as I have been – indeed, as I am, with Mr. Weston. Believe me, Emma. It can come true!"

Emma did not find time to wonder if Mrs. Weston's heart had indeed been broken when she was a young woman, and before she had come to take up her post at Hartfield. As with Mr. Knightley, the presence of Miss Taylor – as she had been – was as enduring and necessary to the very foundations of existence, as the stones and roof tiles of Hartfield itself. There was a need, however, to disabuse the dear friend Mrs. Weston was now become, of the illusion that Jane

Fairfax suffered at losing Frank Churchill.

"She may believe herself heart-broken," cried Emma, "but there is another danger come into poor Jane's life – I swear there is! And we must make sure we save her from it, so I ask you to believe me in turn, my good Mrs. Weston!"

"Another danger?" said Mrs. Weston, rolling her eyes. "Emma, you were ever the imaginist. You go further than I can happily go with you, I fear. What danger is this?"

Emma, to her mortification, found herself tongue-tied. She could not speak of the Frenchwoman; but in her mind's eye she saw her, and she held hands with Jane Fairfax as she looked over her shoulder and smiled.

"You should think more of yourself, dear Emma," said Mrs. Weston in a quiet tone – for the Abbey doors were heard to open, and there was little doubt Mr. Knightley had returned from the yew drive, and from the exchanging of pleasantries with Mrs. Elton. "I mean to say,—" and here the old governess lowered her voice considerably, "have you not, my love, thought of starting on a family yourself? You have cared for your nephews and nieces two years now; the whole village remarks on your kindness and patience. You speak of a school, at Hartfield. Would it not be better by far if you had a child of your own, Emma? Think of schools later. There, I have brought it all out, and I did not intend to fill your mind with such thoughts, when you have the dinner party here tomorrow—"

"And I wish you could come!" said Emma, for she in her own way was as resolute as Mrs. Weston, when it came to choice of a topic between them. That of bringing a child into the world was not a topic ever embarked on or followed by Emma. She could not give the reason— it was very probable that the existence of five orphans of Isabella's whom she felt it right to educate and protect deterred her; deeper reasons she refused at each opportunity to explore. And perhaps the knowledge that Highbury looked to her to provide an heir to Donwell Abbey gave her an added obstinacy on the subject. Henry, John's eldest son, had long been marked down, to succeed as landowner at Donwell; Emma would not disinherit him for the world. This she gave as brief reply to Mrs. Weston, who sighed, and looked away.

"So tell me of the danger to Jane Fairfax, then," said Mrs. Weston, "for I see your need to confide it, Emma. Why, I do not believe I have seen you so agitated since Old Abdy brought round a dolls' house he had made with his own hands – on your fifth birthday, my dear! Tell me – pray!"

Emma, speaking with many pauses and hesitations at first, began a description of the Baroness, and of the undoubted temptation her company held for Jane

Fairfax, bereft as the wretched young woman was of male company. She had no bright prospect; nor anything more from the suitor who had instead married an heiress, than a bouquet of wilting flowers gathered from the hedgerows.

"I fear the Baroness has designs on Jane," murmured Emma; at this moment the door to the drawing-room opened and Mr. Knightley came in, and she blushed scarlet. "That is enough, dear friend, let us talk of other things!"

Mr. Knightley came forward, and placed himself in his accustomed wing chair. His mien was grave, both Emma and Mrs. Weston were not slow to note. Emma, who had expected him to tease her, did not know whether to be thankful or sorry to see him so downcast.

"I must make my way to Randalls," said Mrs. Weston. "I have my little Adelaide awaiting – she must learn her numbers, or she will be as dim-witted as an uneducated child can be." Leaning down, she patted Emma's head. "Tell me more when next I come to the Abbey, my love – on the subject of your dangerous Baroness—"

"Her name is Delphine," said Emma; but then she flushed again, for she had not meant to speak further of the Frenchwoman in the presence of Mr. Knightley.

"Well, I am happy to place the charming Baronne next to brother John tomorrow," said Mr. Knightley; but the attempt at good humour in his tone failed, and Emma saw he was really angry or sad – the two had a way of mingling, with Mr. Knightley.

"Delphine—" said Mrs. Weston, and she appeared to muse a while, before picking her bag from the table and making for the door. "And what do you say is the life story of this remarkable young woman?"

"She has a fortune, so I am told. I shall certainly place her next to my brother," said Mr. Knightley, still in an attempt at jocularity. "That is enough for us, I am sure, Mrs. Weston!"

"She did not find herself the victim of a passion for a young man intended for her protégée, a Mademoiselle Mathilde?" enquired Mrs. Weston, her voice by the door so low as to be almost inaudible. "His name Léonce? No, it cannot be."

"But it is!" Emma leapt to her feet; Mr. Knightley gazed up in mild astonishment at her. "It is one and the same, Mrs. Weston! Tell me more of her – and do you consider I am right – when it comes to Jane Fairfax—?"

"Don't imagine I am happy to hear that there are more concerns over Jane Fairfax," cried Mr. Knightley; and he gave a loud groan. "Has she not had her share of compassion, Mrs. Weston? Do not you agree? Emma thinks too much of her – is not that the case?"

Mrs. Weston, who appeared suddenly to find that she had over-stayed the amount of time she had permitted herself at the Abbey, bustled to the door at an unusual speed. She would not look directly at Emma – but crossed the hall rapidly, and opened the outer door.

"Please, Mrs. Weston—" cried Emma; but she knew she sounded as plaintive as the child or pupil of Mrs. Weston's once had been. That she was Mr. Knightley's wife now must stiffen her resolve, not to think further of the danger she felt still all around her. She was mistress of Donwell Abbey and must not comport herself as a young girl would, to whom everything was fresh, shocking and new.

"My dearest Emma," said Mr. Knightley as they walked back to the drawing-room after Mrs. Weston had taken her leave, "I do not like to blame or censure you. Heaven knows I do not—"

Emma knew the rest. She stood erect; but as she faced the squire, her spouse, she knew in her heart she did not do right to defend her actions of the afternoon.

"As I learnt very lately that you have given leave to young Abdy's sister to occupy the barn, I did not countermand your wishes," said Mr. Knightley; but he sounded more than ever disappointed and weary as he spoke. "I can only hope my misgivings will prove to be unfounded – as must you."

And with that, he was gone.

17

The night which followed was too warm to permit sleep; and too windless to prevent each movement, as it came from Mr. Knightley's room, from being heard; but Emma, drawing back the curtains at the windows and returning to lie with scant comfort on her bed, did not go to him. He might open and close drawers; go to his wardrobe and thence to his writing-table, as often as he pleased. If Emma did not sleep, then nor should he. Only a thunderstorm, when it could be heard to approach far off in the Surrey hills, might bring the comfort both required – though in their very separate ways.

Emma could not forgive Mr. Knightley for what she perceived as his worldly scheme to marry his brother to a fortune – when the poor man, as even Mrs. Weston, the most matrimonially-minded of her friends, had agreed, must be allowed his period of mourning to continue for as long as he required. If he were to be introduced to a potential bride – why, John Knightley must meet a woman he had known all his life, a person he had seen as a sister but could now learn to regard with growing devotion and respect. The Baroness was totally unsuitable! How was Mr. Knightley justified in rebuking his Emma for the sin of marrying her friends, when he was prepared to act as matchmaker himself, between an heiress from a dubious, Continental source, and his own kin! It was unthinkable!

Mr. Knightley's restlessness, ever a mark of disapproval on his part – this must be ascribed to his annoyance at his wife's open-handed response to a request from the Abdy family. But was not Emma infinitely superior to *him*, when all she schemed was the material improvement of a wretched young woman: she did not connive at marrying a fallen woman from the stews of Bristol, to anyone at Highbury! No, of this Mrs. Knightley was innocent. A daughter of an old man who had long served Mr. Woodhouse, had need of a roof over her head: was it not more practical of Emma to assuage the agonies of a mendicant such as Miss Abdy than it would be to dream of uniting a widower with five children and a foreign baroness who might well encourage those children to feel love for her, and then abandon them? How would Mr. Knightley feel then, with nephews and nieces on his hands all heart-broken from the sorry mistake their father had made – a mistake aided and abetted by none other than their uncle George? It was beyond anything: Emma would think of it no more.

But all thoughts led back to the Baroness; and as the distant rumbles in the hills increased, Emma found she could think of little else. If only she could discover how Jane Fairfax and this fascinating creature had first met! And how – here Emma sat upright, a bolster balanced precariously against the bedhead, the slender curtains of the four-poster bed moving at last in the first traces of a wind from afar – how could Mrs. Weston know her history? It was inconceivable, that an old friend, the confidante and teacher of Emma's youth, should keep such knowledge from her, in all the days since the arrival of the two young women at the Vicarage. Was it not a romantic, even a disturbing story?— a beautiful young girl, taken as the bride of a Baron, then widowed before she had time even to see herself as wed – then, the generosity, in promising a marriage portion to a girl as far from finding the satisfactions of nuptials as poor Jane Fairfax now – was it not inevitable that the intended groom should fall in love with the benefactress of his betrothed? Would not anyone who came into contact with the lovely Elise – or Delphine – be as passionately enamoured of her?

As I am, murmured Emma to herself; then, cheeks burning, she leapt from her bed and ran to the open window – for lightning came; and, a very short time after, thunder directly overhead, before the black clouds parted to reveal a full, unmoving moon.

She did not know what she said. She was feverish, it was the abrupt change in the weather which had brought it on. If Emma had known a mother she would have called her now; instead, she resorted to phrases of Mrs. Weston, and she summoned childhood scenes of illness.— For it was true, her body burned now, as her face had just done. She was ill; with an illness that had come as suddenly as the storm that raged about the Abbey. She would not disturb Mr. Knightley, for there was silence at last from his room. He slept amongst his sporting prints, with little to occupy his dreams other than his farm, his apple crop in a month's time, and the books he examined every night, balancing one ledger against its neighbour with all the practice of the landowner who is a working farmer on his land.

The moon was swallowed by clouds again, and gave an impression of fleeing from its pursuers, as Emma fled from a progression of her thoughts. A wind as strong as any that had come to Donwell and its sheltered valley in the month of August followed the thunder and lightning and grasped the small trees newly planted in Mr. Knightley's orchards, and twisted them so they shook. Haystacks in Robert Martin's fields became frisky; wisps flew in the lime walk; and branches of hazel nut bushes were flung as far afield as the lawn below Emma's window, from the hedge which divided the Abbey from Abbey Mill Farm. The night was wild; there was no place to go, but to return to bed.

This Emma did; and it was to lie as a child might on the occasion of a first storm, hands over her ears. It was not only the return of the thunderclaps which inspired her dread. The voice of Elise now sounded in the whistling of the wind: low, a foreign voice that brought storms to her neck and down her spine; and, wherever her hands might roam to hold it at bay, her very soul.

Part Three

18

The next day opened bright and calm. Emma slept late, and was woken by her maid with enquiries from Mrs. Hodges, as to the ability of Mrs. Bates to chew on hard pastry: would not a fricassee be a better dish; the veal was come; would madam kindly instruct?

The sound of Mr. Knightley and his brother came up the stairs to the bedchamber where Emma, unusually tardy in her morning toilet, sent her maid away miserable and sat long at her dressing-table, contemplating in the glass a face she had not seen look back at her since her father's death: pale, wan, pinched with the sadness that had come in the night and would not go away. Mr. Knightley, crossing the hall to the library, spoke with his habitual evenness, and, it seemed to Emma, louder than was his wont, as if to reassure her that the storms of the night were passed. He called his dogs; she heard him inform John that the water bailiff awaited them, and the lake would need draining before any profit could be got from it, or even personal pleasure and enjoyment.— "Though I hope we will be able to sell the fish we catch there, brother John," he added, and then the door to the library was closed behind them. Before it did so, Emma thought she heard the mention of roach, and char, and of the stocking of the lake with brown trout, which the good people of Surrey would buy in quantities.

Not for the first time, Emma reflected on the kindness and consideration of her husband; but today, she thought of these qualities from a distance: they belonged to a stranger. Mr. Knightley would do his best for his brother's inheritance. The lake would yield fresh fish, in this inland part of the country.

There would be a boating party: it would be a fine thing, to go on the water— but for Emma, as her thoughts pursued and tormented her, there was no thought but of the sea.

The sea – which Emma had never visited – had surely been the setting for the meeting between the Baroness and Jane Fairfax. The two women were bound one to the other, she suspected – she felt she knew as much by now; and, just as the truth that had come to her in the night was banished from her mind, so it was replaced by a desire more urgent than any she had ever known, to ascertain where they had first encountered each other.— And, which was as important, indeed essential to Emma's peace of mind, how the story of the beautiful Elise had come to be known to Mrs. Weston. Elise – Delphine – why did the intriguing creature have two names?

Emma, as she sat long at her dressing-table, thought of the marriage she had entered into with Mr. Knightley. She reflected that it was indeed the case that the interests of others had from the very beginning taken precedence over their own. Had they not, at the time of their betrothal, announced they would take a tour of the seaside, a wedding journey, no more than a fortnight's absence from Hartfield? Had not John and Isabella given their word they would come to care for Mr. Woodhouse while Emma and Mr. Knightley, for so many years close to being perceived as brother and sister in the eyes of the world, celebrated their union as man and wife by the ocean, which Emma had never in all her life found the opportunity to see? But one of the Knightley nephews or nieces – indeed, it had been Bella, ever sickly, while little Emma enjoyed the perfect health and bloom of her aunt – had fallen ill in London. The John Knightleys did not come. The wedding journey had been postponed; Mr. Woodhouse grew nervous, when it was proposed again a month later; Emma and her spouse began and continued their married life beneath her father's roof at Hartfield.

Was it this, Emma pondered long, which had continued the union of Mr. Knightley and Miss Woodhouse in the same vein as it had been since she could remember, as a child? With George the uncle of his brother John's children, as they increased in number and he aged, a bachelor; and Emma their young aunt? Was it the failure to take a journey away from Mr. Woodhouse that accounted for Mr. Knightley's enduring propensity to blame and praise her, however he might try to rid himself of the habit? Was it because the couple had remained in her father's house – though the responsibility was theirs, to care for him – which had kept the temperature of the marriage low? They were friends; they *were* brother and sister; Emma, with the greatest bitterness she had known, saw it all now.

So the image of the never-visited sea obtruded yet again, and of two women, both lovely, but one of a great and sensational beauty, as they stood on Weymouth sands. Poor Jane, thought Emma; she will need to find a husband soon if she is to elude the advances of this woman from across the sea. And she smiled at herself for the first time that day, in the glass that had been her husband's mother's – just as this bedchamber, where

Emma slept always unaccompanied, had been Mrs. Knightley's own. She smiled, because she knew she must discover instantly how Mrs. Weston had come to be apprised of the secrets of the Frenchwoman's life; and that she would go to Randalls now, whether the arrangements for the dinner were delayed or no. Emma smiled also, because, if there was one thing she hated, it was concealment and secrecy. And, while visiting Mrs. Weston, she might come to understand – or so she dimly felt – not just the truth of the friendship between Jane Fairfax and the Baroness d'Almane, but also the secrets of her own heart.

19

It was not so simple an accomplishment, to leave a house such as Donwell Abbey when a dinner party was in preparation, as the mistress of the Abbey might have hoped.

There came a further plea for guidance from Mrs. Hodges on the subject of pastry, and Mrs. Bates's teeth, last described at some length by Miss Bates on the occasion of an afternoon visit, where rock cakes had been served along with the lemonade, and which had threatened to extract the old lady's remaining specimens; to this Emma had replied, with all the placid assurance of one who thinks of little but the dental predicaments of her guests, that the pastries should be made as light as possible. She wished to demonstrate to a French visitor to Highbury that pastry was not an art exclusively reserved for the Gallic race: if necessary, Mrs. Hodges should try her hand at *mille feuilles* and *vol-au-vent*, and place chicken in a béchamel sauce between the exquisitely thin wafers.

As she reached the hall, there came Mr. Knightley from the library: however softly Emma walked, she knew he sensed her as she passed; and, if she might like him for it on most days, today she uttered a stifled exclamation of annoyance when the door opened and her husband came out, followed by his brother John Knightley. The latter was, as he would be found to be every day, in an explosively ill humour: even his pipe had been extinguished. He held in his hands a thick ledger, which he carried before him like a tombstone.

"My dear Emma," said Mr. Knightley, who did not see the look of anger on his brother's face, as John stood behind him, in the doorway, "I have been meaning for some time now, to give you certain items—" and he stepped forward to take her hand. Unthinkingly, she flinched away from him. "You are correct, to wonder why I have not thought of it before," cried Mr. Knightley, who was quick at first to show his pain at this rebuff; but then covered it over with a step backwards into the library and a disappearance from sight. This move left John Knightley and Emma standing and staring at each other: Emma wished herself at Randalls, if not an hundred miles away from her brother-in-law. But the thought came to her, that any match Mr. Knightley might hope to make, between his brother and the French woman, was doomed to failure from the start. It was laughable, to imagine Elise seeing John Knightley in any favourable sense; and if Emma had found the opportunity to indulge her desire to laugh, she would have done so.

Mr. Knightley reappeared. He frowned at his brother; but, John Knightley being incapable of taking any hint, whether agreeable or otherwise, remained exactly where he stood, his eyes fastened this time on the red leather box, the covering extremely worn and antique, which Mr. Knightley held in his hands. It was evident, even to Emma in her state of preoccupation, that the box had been removed from the safe in the library that very morning, and had lain on the desk between Mr. Knightley and his brother; for John Knightley examined the box with a greedy, almost menacing air; and at one point it seemed probable that he would lay down his ledger and make a petulant demand for old Mrs. Knightley's jewel casket and its contents.

This was what it was though Emma had seen it only once, just before she was married and installed at Donwell Abbey. Mr. Knightley, smiling in a very fatherly fashion, had warned her playfully not to try to enter the safe – "but the jewels that are here, loveliest Emma, were my mother's, and will henceforth be yours"; and only a complete lack of interest in baubles and decorations on the part of Mr. and Mrs. Knightley both, had resulted in the family heirlooms remaining where they were during all of the four years since the marriage of the squire of Donwell to Miss Woodhouse. Indeed, Emma had worn the tiara on her wedding day – she recalled a very fine strand of pearls, which had also graced her bridal dress – but there had been a dearth of occasions, ever since, at Highbury, that called for the wearing of jewellery— and, as Emma did not care to emulate the customs of Mrs. Elton – there had been none at which she would have felt comfortable with the grandeur and old-fashioned settings of old Mrs. Knightley's gems.

"For our party tonight, dear Emma," said Mr. Knightley, who saw Emma smile at him – for she felt ashamed of her clear desire to escape the purlieus of the Abbey; and now, for the first time in her life, desired to conceal her real wishes from him. "It occurred to me – as we are so many at dinner – you might like to wear the pearls – and indeed, so I am told, pearls are in need of constant contact with the lovely skin of the wearer—" He broke off, and, also unusually for him, he blushed. John Knightley, who muttered something to the effect that his Isabella could well have worn the pearl necklace if there had been no use for it at the Abbey, now at last took his leave; bearing his ledger, he made his way to his room. Emma could do little but pretend relief at being left alone with Mr. Knightley; this did not prevent her from reflecting that something was afoot between the brothers, which had resulted in bad blood; and she could not help feeling that John Knightley had indeed demanded the jewellery to which he, as younger son, had no right in the family estate; while his brother George, in refusing him, had resolved to present it to Emma, as an irrevocable step.

"You say nothing, dearest Emma," said Mr. Knightley, his face still exhibiting the signs of anxiety she had seen there before. Did he fear she had no need of him; that, like a child who has learnt to weather a storm, she had found calm within, despite the tempests of the night before? How little he knows me, Emma thought; and then was forced, from the sheer need for honesty that was ever in her nature, to amend this: how little he knows me *now*. My thoughts were not with him: indeed, he does know his Emma well enough to sense their absence since the return from the walk to the Abdys' cottage, and the Vicarage. And I go walking again, Emma's musings continued; yet my journey does not concern Mr. Knightley or the Donwell Abbey estate one jot. She felt no guilt at this, as she remembered how she had suffered a strange absence of guilt, or of concern for her life, in the wildest passage of the storm.

"You shall choose a new setting – this diadem will look fine in your hair, Emma," said Mr. Knightley, lifting an arc of stones, dull with disuse, from the velvet interior of the box. "But for tonight, I hope and trust you will wish to wear the pearls. Say you will, Emma, it would have given pleasure to my mother. You will be the cynosure of all eyes."

Emma saw he fumbled, and blushed again as he pulled the strand from its resting place; and the thought came to her irresistibly that Mr. Knightley was no longer young: she thought of a painting, or a cartoon, where an elderly admirer with his gouty hands tries in vain to fasten a clasp at a young beauty's neck.

"And where do you go, at this early hour?" continued Mr. Knightley; Emma detected a note in his voice that was distinctly arch. He cannot show his fear of losing my affection for him, she thought; but no answering compassion came. With a coolness of which she would not have been capable even two days back, she replied that she went to Randalls; the day promised to be hot; and she had every wish to go there and back across the fields, before the lack of shade would send her into the woods, where she had no desire to go. "You are right, Emma," said Mr. Knightley gravely; "you have not forgot the gypsies which came to plague poor Harriet Smith when she went walking there. At this time of year, however Larkins may try to keep them out, they do return; and I would not have you frightened by the ruffians, for anything."

Emma could not answer that her fear of the seclusion of the woods lay in a fear of her own, newly-discovered and unowned passion: she would not walk alone with a certain person.— She felt the spring of the overhanging branch, as it touched her face. She felt the change to lips, dry and hot, that came close to hers and brushed her cheek. She must walk in open fields.

"Why do you not take Harriet with you this morning, my dear?" said Mr. Knightley. It was as if some part of his mind was conscious of the battle which waged inside his wife; and he tried both to fight and to assuage it.

Emma shook her head. She could have smiled, to be reminded of her friendship with mild little Harriet Martin: why, once she had attempted to marry the girl to every bachelor in Highbury; but had she not herself found happiness in those soft blue eyes? Where was that feeling now? She was hard put to recall it, she must own.

Yet, as Mr. Knightley spoke, Harriet Martin did indeed materialise, at the tall oak door to the Abbey, and linger on the flagstones, uncertain whether or not she might come in; and for a moment Emma suspected her husband of summoning her, so that thoughts of another might be banished before they could take a stronger hold. But this idea she banished in turn: Harriet came of her own free will; she was walking in the direction of

Randalls, for she had some ribbon she knew would do very well for Mrs. Weston's adorable little girl; "and I am not of an age to wear such a pale pink, Mrs. Knightley," cried the artless creature, holding up a length of the pastel ribbon to her face. "My husband dear Robert does not say so, but I know you will agree; this ribbon is for a child, is that not so?"

Emma did not know how to reply. Harriet seemed indeed a child, as she stood and simpered in the hall. How Emma could have spent so many hours in her company was a puzzle, indeed.

"Now you have a shady walk, Emma!" cried Mr. Knightley; and Emma knew he was relieved for other reasons than the lack of sun on her fair skin. "Off you go, the two of you," he persevered, with a greater show of confidence. "I will see you, Emma, at midday, I have no doubt. There are arrangements – new arrangements – and you have not seen the half of them, my dear."

Emma had no way of imagining to what Mr. Knightley might refer. He had made his habitual face, on having to move his mother's table from the library to the dining-room – but it was still in place, and she assumed he would make a great deal of the move once again, and exact a placement of the guests from her, before moving the larger and smaller chairs, which were as much a part of the old Abbey as was the Knightley family itself. Emma, with a show of friendship, assured both Mr.

Knightley and Harriet Martin that she would not be gone many hours.

"But I go alone," she said, and with an unaccustomed sharpness, which she was unable to prevent; and which, as she saw, offended poor Harriet as deeply as Mr. Knightley had a short time earlier been hurt to the quick. "I go so fast. I am taller than you, dear Harriet, and with longer legs—"

No amount of excuses could dissuade Mr. Knightley and Mrs. Martin from standing by the Abbey door with long faces, as she went. Emma reflected that she had never felt so trapped, as she was today: watched, wondered over; wanted back in the home. For this reason she increased her pace. A sun even hotter than the one of the day before gathered in strength as she walked across the fields; there was no sign of last night's storm; and the leaves on the trees in the woodland which bordered Mr. Knightley's fields were turning to a brown and orange already, in the drought.

She did not turn once, to see if she was still perceived, and within ten minutes the roof of Randalls came into sight – as did Mr. Weston himself, as robust and genial as the bright day which sent him out to inspect his small acreage, on the edge of the Abbey fields.

20

Great was Emma's desire to escape Mr. Weston, however often he repeated he was back much earlier than he had expected, from London; and delighted to find her here. She found to her shame that she searched for a ruse in order to rid herself of him – as she had Mr. Knightley and Harriet, on the steps of Donwell. Here, however, the plea of a superior fastness of movement would not do the trick; for it was at Randalls that Emma wished to remain, until her questions on the subject of the Baroness were answered; it was more a matter of feigning the need for remaining stationary than the contrary, which occupied Emma's imaginings.

"I daresay you are a little disconcerted, Mrs. Knightley," Mr. Weston began, before Emma could confront him with the absolute necessity of going in to the house to find his wife, bringing her out, and leaving them both alone here. "You must think my son a peculiarly heartless young man.— No, I will take no polite denial. You think ill of Frank, dear Emma, for breaking the heart of Jane Fairfax, and finding the temerity to visit us here while she stays at the Vicarage. Let me assure you that the little party from Enscombe set off without the least idea that Miss Fairfax would be at Highbury! Poor Frank went quite green when my wife was constrained to pass the information to him, upon arrival."

Emma in turn gave her assurances that she had no reproaches to make to Mr. Weston's son. "Frank had every good reason to wish to come to Randalls, to visit his father and his new mother—"

"It is four years," said Mr. Weston; and his genial manner for a moment lessened; then, seeing the advantage in the period of time that had elapsed since his only son's last visit – and the implications, that marriage to an heiress in the North was as demanding as sustaining the role of nephew to the late Mrs. Churchill had been – he brightened once more, and began again on the subject. But Emma, thinking she saw a corner of Mrs. Weston's dress by the west side of the house, going into the conservatory latterly erected there, held her hand high and arrested Mr. Weston in his flow.

"I do not believe that Jane Fairfax suffers," said she in as grave a tone as she could muster; she, also, smiled at the prospect, such a very short time away, of having dear Mrs. Weston to herself. She would be told the full history.— For Emma, the burning curiosity of the passionate was new; the thirst in need of quenching instantly, for all her life she had known the details, intimate and public, of the man she married in Highbury church, and the story of the Baroness was as an unread book: highly commended, the details of the plot known to her friend, and shortly to be passed on! It was an intoxicating thought; and Mr. Weston, understanding as little as Mr. Knightley had done, responded only to the gaiety and radiance his visitor gave off. This was all he had, to prompt him to produce his next words to her.

"It is time we arranged a dance, Emma," said Mr. Weston accordingly. "And not to be held at the Crown Inn this time, my dear. Do not you agree that our conservatory, lit by candles and leading directly from the dining-room, would hold upward of fifty? Indeed, Frank does: he has not changed, when it comes to dancing, I may assure you, Mrs. Knightley!"

Emma did now increase her pace in the direction of that glass edifice. She expected Mr. Weston's habitual remark, that Donwell Abbey would do very well with a conservatory; and this duly came; but after it came further a sign of Mr. Weston's continuing preoccupation with the hard-hearted behaviour of his son. For politeness' sake, Emma arrested her progress by the side of the house; the conservatory walls were in view, and within them a handsome arrangement of ferns and hanging baskets, each with its crown of tropical plants. There was reason to go in here, as Mr. Weston was a frequent visitor to Kew when on one of his trips to London, to look after his interests; and there was always a new specimen to be appraised and wondered at. Today, as Emma had glimpsed, Mrs. Weston had entered there, and would give out her exotic tale, much as an orchid or lily gives its heady scent. The life of the Baroness would be unfurled.

"You say Jane Fairfax does not suffer," said Mr. Weston in a low voice, as Emma, peering around the corner, saw a figure in a wide-brimmed straw hat in a far chair by the windows that looked south from the conservatory, over the rolling hills and land that was all in Donwell Abbey's demesne. "Can you furnish any proof – Oh my dear, we have often mistaken the intentions and results of Frank's attachments, as you know—"

Mr. Weston broke off; but Emma felt further shame, that she could not bring greater evidence of Jane's recovery from her treatment at the hands of the notorious Frank Churchill. It was true, as she reflected, that Mr. Weston did not know how to measure his son's affections: he had thought Emma herself might be heart-broken, when Jane's engagement to his son became known! Emma did not like to think of it. She searched for words of comfort; but she did not wish to admit that her proof was scant: she had a feeling that Jane and the Baroness were closely allied, and she wished Jane would announce a betrothal, before the summer was out; that was all she knew. With John Knightley so far removed from possibility, she could only hint to Mr. Weston that another, not so far removed from Frank Churchill, might well be the one to lead the lovely Miss Fairfax down the aisle of St. Mary's, Highbury.

"Captain Brocklehurst?" Mr. Weston's voice grew loud, in his surprise – and Emma feared his wife heard him, for there was a stirring from the figure by the conservatory window. Mrs. Weston must not come out here: she must tell the Baroness's story in private: Emma cursed her judgement, and wished she had said nothing at all.

"He is Frank's brother-in-law, you know," said Mr. Weston in an extremely doubtful tone. "This would make Miss Fairfax all the more unhappy, would it not?"

At this point, and greatly to Emma's relief, a servant came from the house to say the head gardener awaited Mr. Weston within; and, murmuring his apologies, the good man left.

Emma, deciding she would walk around the outside windows of the conservatory and surprise her friend there, smiled gleefully and set off. She saw the fuchsias, in bright clusters, which grew in the company of geraniums, within the glass; beyond, where a palm tree drooped its graceful fronds, was the loved, familiar figure of Miss Taylor – of Mrs. Weston as she had long been, though as governess and almost as mother is how Emma was accustomed to think of her. She sat patiently, as if becalmed by the tranquil view now afforded at Randalls with the construction of the glass house.

Emma went on tiptoe; she felt the conspiracy, and the joy of herself as a child, when she had been Miss Taylor's pupil and her cherished charge. She pressed her face against the pane, and looked in.

Captain Mark Brocklehurst, in a white, floating gown and with cheeks and lips rouged to a bright hue, sat in the wicker wing chair, under a wide-brimmed straw hat. Emma gasped, and with her foot dislodged a stone in the gravel path where she stood; he looked round, and saw her there.

Emma turned and fled. She saw Mr. Weston emerge from the house, and she tried to slow her run. But she was able to see, when once she twisted round in her headlong flight, that her host, unable to decide whether to arrest her in her path or carry into his conservatory a new plant, tall and trembling in an earthenware pot, allowed expediency to make his choice; and he took the latter course. That he entered his glass construction to find himself quite alone, was certainly the case: Emma, stopping altogether this time at the edge of the lawn at Randalls, saw inside the conservatory entirely from this new vantage point. It was empty. Alerted by an unexpected visitor, the Captain had fled, as she had done, and was nowhere to be seen.

21

*L*yme. We first met at Lyme. We had taken the children from Weymouth. We were there two days. It was very fine."

These were the words which were lodged in Emma's memory; and even though they had been uttered but a half hour back, she felt already that a great span of time had passed since their utterance, by Jane Fairfax. She had hoped for more; but the governess, more reserved even than in the days before her employment by Mrs. Smallridge, would vouchsafe nothing further. Emma saw a figure on the Cobb – her sister Isabella, who had once visited Lyme, had told her of that stone rampart, which juts out over the sea there, and is frequently drenched with spray.— Emma saw the Baroness, an isolated and splendid figure, as she stood cloaked and drenched, by the encroaching sea. But, in the end, there was still no answer to the mystery of the Frenchwoman. If she stood on the Cobb, how had she come from France? Would she return to Lyme? Had she friends or family there?— Jane Fairfax, as was her custom, would not be drawn. Emma found it disgusting, in the extreme. The only solace was the presence of the Baroness at the table: Emma was aware that all eyes were upon the beautiful foreigner, and that her own must not linger too long there. She moved her regard, as a hostess should; and concluded that the guests were well attended at Donwell Abbey tonight.

There was a new dining-table. But the shame, for Emma, of noticing nothing changed at the Abbey upon her return from Randalls, stood in the way of a full appreciation of Mr. Knightley's gesture. His mother's table need no longer be carried in, if they were more than six people for dinner! It had needed him, to say it; and John Knightley, standing as he habitually did, directly behind his brother, had muttered that good money was spent easily at Donwell, and the results not seen or liked by the mistress of the house.

There were also the pearls – which Emma felt at her neck, loose, for her throat was more slender than old Mrs. Knightley's had been – but constricting nevertheless. She could not look across the table and see the

Baroness there. She smiled at Mr. Knightley and touched the necklace; and he smiled in gratification. It was a pitiful business, Emma thought, and she found herself wishing she was an hundred miles distant from the Abbey, and from him, tonight.

There had not been time to think of what she had seen, at Randalls. All Emma could do, as she glanced at the dinner-table, which was fashioned from satinwood and was of the new type, which was marquetry, was to understand that Jane Fairfax must marry John Knightley and nobody else. There could be no wedding with Captain Brocklehurst. She shied away from the memory of the vision of the handsome young man, as she had seen him, and wondered at the meaning of it all. But Jane and Frank Churchill's brother-in-law could not be man and wife. As for the gallant Captain's admiration of herself – Emma found to her annoyance that she was piqued. She had not fancied him so much in love with her as truly taken by her beauty and her wit; after all, he had practised a deception. The Captain was not what he seemed. Emma felt, in her imaginings, that she had saved poor Jane Fairfax from a dreadful fate; and wondered at the unfortunate young woman's lack of gratitude at her benefactress's efforts on her behalf.

Instead, the object of Emma's charity sat very still and pale beside Mr. Knightley's brother. Emma could have kicked her, to provoke some kind of movement; but

John was himself much taken with his neighbour on the other side, the Baroness; and if Emma saw her husband's good humour improve by the minute, it was doubtless due to the instant success of his matchmaking. It was too provoking – so Emma was bound to conclude – to be borne.

Good, if unexpected aspects of the guests had otherwise revealed themselves at dinner in the Abbey; and, to provide calm for her tormented soul, Emma attempted to recall them and to give them their due. Mrs. Elton, despite a gown of purple satin and an assortment of brooches and ear-rings, kept quieter than was her wont: the Knightley pearls, as she named Emma's strand, on perceiving it around her hostess's neck, had thrown her into a reflective state; and, apart from references to the silver at the Sucklings' house near Bristol, and her own forthcoming visit to that family, she was silent. Emma found she had much to be thankful for, here. Mrs. Elton would have been insufferable, if she had been in full voice; and her husband, accustomed as he was by now to await her lead in all matters conversational, made no more sound than a domestic animal which has been encouraged on occasion to give a growl of disapproval or a whine of joy.

Mrs. Smallridge, apart from a need – as Emma soon discovered – to be thanked at every opportunity, whether she passed down the sauce-boat, referred to her generosity with candles in the schoolroom, or wished the company to recall her rapid discovery of Mrs. Knightley at the time of her visit there, in the Vicarage garden, was easily distracted by the most commonplace of dinner-party talk. She sat at Mr. Knightley's left hand; and was fed by him with information on the history of the Abbey and its ancient bounds. Her questions – for which she expected also praise and thanks – were as frequent as gunfire. Mr. Knightley did his best. But then, as Emma reflected with some bitterness, a conversation with Mrs. Smallridge kept him from taking up the time and attention of his other neighbour – who was the Baroness. The romance with John Knightley could bloom, as Mrs. Smallridge explored the Abbey's past.

Most of all to be glad for was the apparent improvement of Miss Bates. She had come with her mother. Emma owned herself quite moved, for Mrs. Bates's dinners with Mr. Woodhouse had been a prominent feature of her father's life. That the lady cried out in delight at the promise of baked apples brought laughter and a sense of compassionate friendship to the table; and that Emma had remembered to produce just the biscuits old Mrs. Bates had enjoyed at Hartfield was much remarked upon – though Mrs. Smallridge, scenting that thanks were given in a direction not her own, demanded gratitude in advance by declaring she would herself take a batch of newly-baked biscuits twice a week to Miss Bates's house, and would have done so already, if she had known what Mrs. Bates's favourites were. Emma was hard put not to laugh, at this attempt to put her in the wrong, for not telling a guest of Mrs. Elton the tastes of a lady previously unknown to her. This was the kind of nonsense produced by the party: anyone said anything; and biscuits were less harmful than most topics introduced at a dinner-table.

Miss Bates did speak – it would have been odd indeed, if she had not – but Emma noticed that she spoke with greater clarity than usual. Her only aberration lay in the repetition of the last word – or last few words – of the sentence just uttered by the other person, with whom she was engaged in conversation; and, as Emma reflected with a good degree of relief, it was improbable in the extreme that words not said in polite society would be aired here.

All in all, the evening at Donwell brought out the best in everyone – if Emma could bring herself to overlook the roaring good humour of John Knightley, at being seated next to the Baroness. She knew herself at fault, in blaming the poor widower for enjoying himself on one of the rare festive occasions which he had no choice but to attend. She must bask in the sense of a dinner that was delicious, and well presented; she must feel she did good, and brought happiness to Miss Bates and her mother, as well as to those who were less deserving; and there would be appreciation later, without doubt, from Mr. Knightley. Emma had no one to blame but herself, if she was miserable at finding her curiosity on the subject of the Baroness unsatisfied. She knew she must smile, and not look across at her; and in both of these resolutions she succeeded – until the meal was almost at an end.

Mrs. Elton spoke of the seaside, and of a journey she intended to make there: she and her party from the Vicarage were due to set out in less than a week, and to stay several more; the destination was none other than Lyme – whence, as Emma had with difficulty extracted from Jane Fairfax, the Baroness had been discovered and brought first to Weymouth and hence, with the Smallridge children, to Highbury.

"The Sucklings have taken a house there, just above the Cobb, with the Bragges, you know! Indeed, it is a house which has been in the family of Lady Carinthia Bragge for many generations. Will it not be salubrious – the air is so fine there, so I am told? And the *chère Baronne* – she informs us her own very dear maman and papa were accustomed to visit Lyme, before the – *ah, hélas*! – Baronne, forgive me, do!"

Mrs. Elton's mention, as Emma presumed of the Revolutionary terror and thus of the cruel method of death suffered by the parents of the Baroness, caused her to look straight across the table; which resulted in the discovery that Jane Fairfax and the Baroness looked at each other behind John Knightley's back, before resuming a serious contemplation of their forks and spoons.

"Mrs. Knightley – you will make such a difference to the party if you consent to come," cried Mrs. Elton. Her husband gave a sound which was a conjunction of a growl and a whine: it was probable that he did not know the degree of sincerity of his wife's remark. "Please, *chère Baronne*, persuade our lovely hostess to accompany us to the seaside! For she will give the greatest pleasure to poor Jane, if she consents: and I do believe also, that Mrs. Knightley may have visited the outlying estates of Donwell Abbey an hundred times, but she has never seen the sea!"

"It was I who prised that information from Mrs. Weston," put in Mrs. Smallridge. "When I went to her to ask for the loan of school books to replace those left by you at Weymouth, Jane, is that not correct?"

"Yes, and I thank you, Mrs. Smallridge," replied Jane Fairfax in a low voice.

"So must we ask Knightley if he will not make up for the loss of a wedding journey to the seaside all of four years ago?" demanded Mrs. Elton. "Can Knightley not spare a day or two away from the management of his estates? We have heard a great deal of this lake, just returned to the family lands. But no expedition has been promised us there. Why, when my *caro sposo* and I visit Maple Grove, we are never without a trip here or there, at least every two or three days. Is that not so, Mr. Elton? Philip, dear, we await your reply."

The vicar, who had been halfway between a growl of corroboration and bark of disparagement at the lack of pleasure trips on the part of the Knightleys, ended with a coughing fit. Mrs. Elton poured him water from a jug.

"I fear I shall not be able to go," said Mr. Knightley. "I have business here. The 'new lake', as you phrase it, Mrs. Elton, is in need of dredging, before any trips, of either a sporting or of a purely pleasurable nature, may take place there. It is, besides, my brother John Knightley's property: I know he invites you all, when the lake is cleared, to join him at a boating party: most of Highbury will be invited."

"Then we will not be amongst them," said Mrs. Elton lightly. "We like to think of ourselves as more exclusive than *that*. No, we shall make do with the sea; and I would in any case far prefer a sailing boat and to go out on the brine, to being on inland water in nothing better than a punt."

"Punt," said Miss Bates in a very loud voice. Emma glanced at her, concerned; but her thoughts were too much on the invitation to Lyme in the company of the mysterious Baroness, to permit her to fret over Miss Bates.

However, Miss Bates was now set off, and could not be stopped. "My dear Mrs. Elton . . . how you are right. Why, the seaside is quite, . . . Yes.— You must ask dear Jane. She has taken the children to Cromer. It is fairyland. Oh, so she says. It is in— Oh dear, I have quite forgot. Jane – assist me here, I beg you—"

"Norfolk," said John Knightley – as he had not uttered a word for some time, and had even permitted that his brother should issue invitations on his part, the table turned to look at him in surprise.

"Isabella would go there, when Mr. Woodhouse wished her to visit Southend," said Mr. Knightley, smiling. "And he takes his children to Cromer still. You do not object?" – this to John – "that we speak of Norfolk?"

"Fuck," said Miss Bates.

22

*L*ong and loud were the repercussions of this
recent discussion of seaside resorts suitable
for widowers, with their children, and of
the beauties and advantages of the coast of Devon, over
that of the flat lands of Anglia (for such was the hubbub
subsequent to Miss Bates's habit of repetition, that
everyone spoke at once; and Mrs. Elton, for the first
time in her life, was quite drowned out).

Some time elapsed, therefore, before Emma could
reasonably suggest the adjournment of the ladies to the
drawing-room, and thus declare the meal at an end.
However great her desire to do so, it would seem too
much of an escape from table – and as Miss Bates was
as apparently unaware of her speech as any child might

have been, to perpetrate a final cruelty on the very daughter and mother for whom the party had been intended, seemed unnecessary indeed. This decision did not, on the other hand, prevent Miss Bates from continuing with her garrulity: the unaccustomed number of people at table, in addition to the very evident difficulties experienced by old Mrs. Bates on encountering a meringue, had kept her unusually quiet until now.

"Yes, Jane has written to me from Norfolk," Miss Bates continued in a blithe tone – as she did so, many at the table shrank back from a reprise, and Emma rose to her feet, and signalled that the ladies should take their leave. Port would be brought in by the footman; Mr. Knightley and his brother, and Mr. Elton would be the only company left in the dining-room. "She was there with the Colonel and Mrs. Campbell," said Miss Bates, who now found herself assisted to her feet by Mrs. Smallridge. "The Colonel, as Jane wrote to me, had taken a pleasant house, as near the sands as you can imagine. The children were so happy—"

"My children do not expect anything less," said Mrs. Smallridge in a tone which demonstrated her awareness of a lack of gratitude on Miss Bates's part, for helping her to her feet. She then went with an officious expression to aid Mrs. Bates – but the old lady, deep in reminiscences of the past with Mr. Knightley, refused to move. "There was. Yes. Oh, Emma – Mrs. Knightley, my dear – I do hope you will ask Jane to play the pianoforte here this evening. She performed for the Colonel, you know – and there was quite a party. Yes. It was sublime. But I say, you have not forgot, Mr. Knightley, I do hope?"

Emma repeated with some emphasis that the ladies must accompany her to the drawing-room. She saw that Mrs. Elton had taken the decision to show offence, at the turn the evening had taken: it would be disagreeable indeed, if the Vicar's wife were to circulate in Highbury unpleasant gossip on the subject of Miss Bates's latest difficulties of articulation.

"It is not safe to keep a pianoforte by the sea," Mrs. Elton however contented herself with. "The keys become damp. It was on the occasion of the Bragges' and the Sucklings' giving a musical evening at Lyme, I may say, that Mrs. Suckling's diamond ring was found to be missing. She was attempting to repair the piano herself, you know – and we all concluded the ring must have fallen down inside! These are the perils of presenting a musical evening at the seaside, Mr. Knightley. You are well advised to stay at home!"

"And only. Yes. Such a host of friends! Oh, there is not anything but the finest dry air in Norfolk, Mrs. Elton—"

"Dear Miss Bates, do accompany us to the drawing-room," said Emma hastily. "I shall ask you to write out your requirements for Donwell apples, this year. Mr. Knightley tells me he sends either too few or too many—"

"Apples and pears! Why, Emma, I dreamt I saw them. On the stairs." Miss Bates here pointed dramatically at John Knightley, and then burst out laughing. "Mr. John Knightley heard my Jane, indeed he did! Is she not a wonderful performer, Mr. Knightley? Indeed!"

John Knightley looked away, and Emma saw that he and Jane Fairfax exchanged glances; but, as disgust was uppermost in her brother-in-law's expression, she had time only to conclude that Miss Fairfax's extreme reserve, coupled with John Knightley's evident dislike of the young woman, had not made it probable that either would make mention of a previous meeting, at Cromer.

Now I know they have already met, the mutual loathing is easier to explain, thought Emma, as she recalled the ill-assorted pair at her first sighting of them on the drive at the Abbey. It is very like Jane Fairfax that she will not confide even this, to one who has her best interests at heart. And not for the first time, Emma wondered at the governess's lack of gratitude towards her. She need never have gone to the trouble of marrying Mr. Knightley's brother and Miss Bates's niece. They hated each other very cordially already.

The drawing-room was finally entered; and here Emma was confronted with a recurrence of the agitation which had possessed her, earlier— for the Baroness, smiling, came to sit at her side – and all the jumping up and settling of old Mrs. Bates; all the offering of lemonade or tea; and all the music-sheet turning in the world, could not prevent a blush from spreading on Emma's cheek and reaching down to her bosom, where she felt a constriction that was almost too painful to bear. There was only one thing to be thankful for; and that was the absence of Mr. Knightley from the room. The gentlemen lingered over their port. Was this not the opportunity for which Emma had yearned? She could ask the Baroness as many questions as she liked.

But Emma found, to her alarm, that she was as dumb as Miss Bates was full of speech, on this important occasion. The Baroness, of whom no enquiries could be made, due to this unprecedented shyness on the hostess's part, sat wordless herself at Emma's side. Finally, as the door opened and Mr. Elton, his confidence and powers of expression restored by Mr. Knightley's port, strode into the room, the beautiful young Frenchwoman turned to Emma – who was, in turn, aware of dark eyes fastened on her with an impish humour, and black brows very strong above them, which lent a note of gravity to a teasing air. Mr. Knightley, following hard on Mr. Elton, entered the drawing-room at this point and looked at the two women on the sofa: they were far from the pianoforte, where Jane Fairfax played, and well removed from Miss Bates, who now sat by her niece in a reverential hush.

"You will come to Lyme?"

These were the Baroness's only words: Emma knew she must treasure them, and investigate and explore their underlying meaning later, when she was alone in bed. Mr. Knightley, who had come up to them with his habitual alacrity, came to stand before his wife and her companion, as if about to deliver a sentence on both ladies; while his brother, with all the force of the legal profession on his side, stood nodding just behind him.

"I would prefer that you do not accompany Mrs. Elton and her party on this expedition, Emma," said he; and John Knightley, placing his hands behind his back, strolled around the sofa where his sister-in-law and the Baroness were placed, as if they were two felons in the dock. "There is much to be done at the Abbey, to keep you here at this time of year," continued Mr. Knightley – who did not, as Emma saw, dare to look her in the eye. "I have informed Mr. Elton just now that you will not be amongst those setting off for the coast in the near future. But my brother and I have agreed to postpone the boating party on the lake to a date agreeable to Mr. and Mrs. Elton – and to allow her the pleasure of picking the guests for John, as he has no wife to do it for him."

"It is well summed up," said John Knightley with

satisfaction, as Emma looked in astonishment, and increasing anger, from one brother to the next. "Though I allow there is a strong probability of stormy weather, by late September. Indeed, I am sure of the equinoctial gales, as evidence has accreted over the centuries—"

Emma rose. She did not cast a look behind her, as she crossed the room, and went to stand by the pianoforte. Despite her own confusion and rage, she was able to note that Jane Fairfax was very pale, and her throat was congested.

The performance was announced to have come to an end. John Knightley, in a whisper that was only too audible, declared himself delighted to hear it. Emma, as she bade her guests farewell, thought him second only to Mr. Knightley in being the most odious man she had ever had the misfortune to know.

23

$\mathscr{E}$mma went to her room. She sat a long time at her dressing-table; the maid did not come; and it was after unclasping the pearls from her throat and letting down her hair, that a knock was heard at the door. Her misery prompted her to call out that it was too late: she was in need of nothing; but that same unhappiness kept her silent. Emma was mortified: she had been exposed as chattel and child together, by Mr. Knightley, before a woman of high birth – to which Emma was ever susceptible – and of a degree of sophistication unknown to Highbury society. Emma and her husband were provincial gentry, laughable figures in a landscape peopled by other fools and dim-wits. She would rather be discovered insensible, than have to confront the Baroness d'Almane again.

Yet, after tapping once more, it was the Baroness who stood in the doorway; and who advanced. Her dark eyes were wide in apprehension; her gown, of a deep red silk, seemed to burn with the force of fire, as she came to Emma, helpless before her as the prey of a predatory bird must find itself, on a dark and moonless night.

There was no question now, of asking of the Frenchwoman's past life. The present – captured in a long, unalterable minute by the turning of the key in the lock, by her nocturnal visitor – sufficed for Emma. The cool hands, of which she had thought – and then dismissed the thought, or fretted on behalf of "poor Jane" at the touch – descended to her shoulders. In the mirror, the black brows, as masculine as the soft cheeks and graceful neck were a woman's, looked back, poised above Emma's own.

They kissed. Emma did not leave the stool where she perched, but permitted the cool, strong hands to run from her shoulders to her neck: the pearls, still hanging loosely at her throat, tumbled to the floor.

"You will come to me."

The Baroness's voice was low. She knelt a moment – not more – Emma heard a roughness in her speech, and wondered at the passion that could not be suppressed, in it. Going as smoothly and soundlessly as she had advanced, Elise was at the door; the key turned; she was gone.

Now appeared the maid. She found her mistress wanton-eyed and wild-haired; she was dismissed, brush in hand, in a tone she had never received from Mrs. Knightley in all her time at Donwell Abbey. The house, trembling – or so it seemed to the girl as she fled down the stairs to Mrs. Hodges – rocked like a boat on a stormy night, beneath her feet. There came the sound of a woman running – running as women of good breeding do not run – and of a cry, so desperate in its longing, its denial and anguish, that the maid was frozen on the back stairs, just a flight above the reassurance of the kitchen, the warmth of lamps and bustle there.

In the library, Mr. Knightley and his brother, closely poring, as was their custom, over accounts and ledgers for the new estates returned to the family, rose as one, and went to the door. The pounding of the feet had passed by them; and there was no repetition of the wailing cry.

"An owl: we must expect an early autumn this year, George," said John Knightley; and he lit up his pipe, which had gone out.

The maid flew in, propelled by William Larkins. It was not her fault. She had gone to old Mrs. Knightley's room, to take another pillow for Mr. Knightley. She did not say more, each reference to the sleeping habits of

Mr. Knightley and his wife must implicate her further; and she had seen, as the stranger unlocked the door and came out, the look on Emma's face: she would not forget it; there had been evil let loose in her bedchamber; this she could confide to Mrs. Hodges and several other maids, if no one else. Besides, William Larkins would dismiss her from employment, if she spoke loosely of the visitor, and of the scene of abandon she had walked in on, then.

Mr. Knightley frowned. He remarked that it was late; but that he would send for Mrs. Weston nevertheless. James should go for her in the carriage, instantly. Mrs. Weston must be reassured, first and foremost, that there had been neither death nor serious misfortune at the Abbey. Emma was in need of her; that was all.

But there had indeed occurred a misfortune, which, when confided to the proprietor of Donwell Abbey, occasioned an outburst of expletives worthy of Miss Bates.

The maid wept once more. She had not seen the pearls had gone, at first. She had searched the dressing-table, the box— but Mrs. Knightley had said nothing—"

"This is most strange!" cried John Knightley, taking on the role of prosecutor; the maid shrank back. "Your mistress must have seen them stolen – I advise you consider again the scene as you witnessed it upon entering Mrs. Knightley's room!"

But the wretched girl could not obey the lawyer, and resorted to piteous sobbing. Mr. Knightley, frowning at his brother, went to comfort her. "There is little doubt as to the identity of the culprit," he remarked to John Knightley, as the girl quietened, and William Larkins was instructed to lead her down to the servants' quarters. "The pearls were taken by Emma's mysterious visitor. Our maid will recall her clothing and appearance, when she grows calm. We must leave Emma in peace – Mrs. Weston must come to her."

24

 ear Emma, it was I who was at fault, that I did not warn you. Forgive me – and let us compose ourselves. It is a bad business; and I would not have Mr. Knightley see you like this – indeed I would not."

Mrs. Weston sat at the end of Emma's bed. Her patient was flushed, and tears ran down her cheeks, very copiously: the very mention of Mr. Knightley brought further sobs; it was as if she heard of his death, or of a great misfortune, indeed. It was impossible, for Mrs. Weston, to bring calm to that most superior of beings, Emma Woodhouse, who was Mrs. Knightley of Donwell Abbey, and esteemed and admired by all Highbury society.

"You came to seek me out," said Mrs. Weston in a low voice, "and I was away from Randalls, my dear child. But I castigate myself now – most severely I do – that I did not come and voice my suspicions to you straight away. I had Frank with me, you know – he is gone back to Enscombe today – Mrs. Churchill says she cannot do without him. The poor boy – he has but to lose an exacting aunt, only to find a wife who demands all the more from him in return for a fortune."

"And Captain Brocklehurst?" said Emma, in a voice still stifled from the grief that had overcome her. Mrs. Weston was here! There was talk of Mr. Perry's being summoned, but it had been expressly forbidden that he should be disturbed at this hour of night – there was a hope for a return to health and sanity for Emma, now her great friend and past governess was come.

"Captain Brocklehurst," said Mrs. Weston, smiling. "Mr. Knightley forbade your visit to Lyme, my dear, because he had heard earlier that Mrs. Elton had invited the Captain to join us – some foolish idea she has, that Jane Fairfax and Frank's brother-in-law will make a match; and with Frank gone to Yorkshire—"

"Mr. Knightley forbade me Lyme because—"

"He was jealous of Captain Brocklehurst," said Mrs. Weston simply. For the first time since the disaster that evening, Emma smiled; then found she could not help herself from laughing. Mrs. Weston laughed also – but whether she saw the handsome young man as Emma had seen him in the conservatory – or was merely entertained at the idea that any Captain, however dashing, could measure up to Mr. Knightley, it was not within Emma's power to ascertain.

"I wished to tell you," continued Mrs. Weston in a whisper, so that her charge – and Emma felt, in this way, as if she had never grown older, as if Mrs. Weston could still cure all her ills – must come up close to her, "I should have told you, that very first time here when you were just back from Mrs. Elton's garden and had met the Baroness—"

Emma shuddered. It was August yet, but a fire had hastily been built since the crime and the desuetude of the Abbey's young mistress had become known. The wood, scented and thus reminiscent of Mr. Knightley, who would come in, fragrant with pine cone and beech, from working in the Abbey woodlands, flickered as it burned at the end of the long room. This bedchamber must not hear the name of the Baroness again: Mrs. Weston, seeing Emma's response to her speaking of her, held her friend in her arms before continuing.

"I did suspect then, Emma. For you see – we have two heroines by the name of Delphine, to contend with, here. Oh, Emma, my child, if you had paid more attention to your books! If you had not flitted from crayon and sketching pad to pianoforte and thence to the library and back again, without giving concentration to each task . . ."

Emma, pulling away from Mrs. Weston, sat upright in the four-poster and her cheeks, white as the "poor Miss Taylor" of earlier days had never seen them, had rings of red at the centre as if daubed there with a brush.

"Delphine is not her name – and she is not a baroness, Emma. Indeed, her name, or so she recounts on occasions—"

"Is Elise!" cried Emma, who relapsed on to the pillows as if she had been shot by another marauder in her bedchamber, this time a bringer of the truth rather than a thief.

"Eliza perhaps," said Mrs. Weston; and she wept, Emma saw; but sympathy had ever dictated the good woman's feelings, and she thought no more of it, then.

"So you must remember, Emma – that Delphine is the name of a book – yes, it is a book so infamous that it has thrown heads of state into discomposure; Delphine, the heroine created by Madame de Staël, and proscribed by the Emperor, though he was powerless, by the time it came into his hands. You were not given the book to read, dear Emma; but we discussed it, and your thoughts, I understand now, were far away when we did so! Passionately in love with Léonce, she flees to Switzerland – from there, once her lover has gone to fight for his country, she roams in wild lands—"

"No. Do not continue!" cried Emma.

"The other *Delphine* was of course written by our mentor, Emma, none other than Madame de Genlis. Why, you remarked that I had named my little Anna Adelaide, after the child she addresses in her delightful tales. You must recall the Baroness d'Almane in those stories—"

"Oh, I do," said Emma, and then fell silent.

There came the sound of the great portals of the Abbey opening, into the hall; and of footsteps, of muffled voices and of the library door, which swung to: Emma saw, in her mind's eye, the mahogany panels as they gleamed in the candlelight from the chandelier, when it was lit in the evenings, and she knew Mr. Knightley came out, alone, to mount the stairs in search of his wife.

"What can I say to him?" she murmured to Mrs. Weston. The sheets were bunched in her hands; her hair, uncombed and disordered, tumbled down her back; the condition of her night-dress, which Mrs. Weston had insisted she put on, was as much a signal of her fever as the bed linen and the untidy room, where those who had searched for the missing pearls had left the mark of their endeavours. "What can I say?" repeated Emma, who was now overcome with a deadly languor.

"You need say nothing at all, dearest Emma," said Mr. Knightley, striding into the room; Emma saw, as she shivered in the chill which now overcame her, that he smiled and held himself very tall. "The criminal is apprehended. By a happy chance, a diamond ring belonging to Mrs. Elton's friend Mrs. Suckling, has been discovered along with other loot. The good lady will have plenty to say tomorrow, I do not doubt, on the subject of the recovery of a gem of such important provenance as Lady Carinthia Bragge!"

Emma pulled herself upright. She did not feel Mrs. Weston's hands, as they pulled at her hair and fitted a lace cap; she did not know a velvet cloak, suitable for the night which had descended on Donwell Abbey, had been placed by her friend, about her shoulders. She stared only at Mr. Knightley.

"Emma, I have never seen you prettier!" Mr. Knightley turned his most good-humoured countenance on Mrs. Weston; and she rose, to go quietly from the room. "My dear, you must rest tonight. Be assured the criminal is caught – the Abdy woman, with all the jewels taken by her accomplice, the *soi-disant* Baroness. My grave misgivings on the subject of Mr. Abdy's daughter proved well-founded, alas: she was caught up in a web of thieves, at Bristol – and our famous Baroness, who was never nearer France than the West Country – Lyme, amongst other places – was a leader of them. She has fled – but she will be caught, I do not doubt it."

Emma, who had her memories of the Frenchwoman's

rough accent to torment her, said nothing.

"Now we may all enjoy some peace. But first, if you will permit me, Emma—"

And for the first time in all the history of their marriage, Mr. Knightley went to kiss his wife, whether she permitted it or not. That she *did*, was evident from the long silence which proceeded from Mrs. Knightley's bedchamber at Donwell Abbey, that night. Even the importunate climbing of the stairs by John Knightley and the subsequent rattle of his legal jargon on the subject of the purloined pearls outside the door, did not disturb the perfect happiness of Mr. and Mrs. Knightley's union.

25

What totally different feelings did Emma bring downstairs the next morning from those with which she had ascended the night before!— Then she had suffered the pangs of humiliation and the agony of an obsession, both – now she was in an exquisite flutter of joy, and a joy of a degree, moreover, as she believed must still be greater when the flutter should have passed away.

She sat down at the round table – how little she had noticed it the night before!— and how often had she looked out at the same shrubs in the lawn and observed the same lovely effect of the eastern sun in the morning!— But never in such a state of spirits, never in anything like it; and it was with difficulty that she summoned enough of her usual self to be the attentive lady of the house, when John Knightley came in; wished for his breakfast; and then was gone again, with not a word of the conversation between them remembered by her.

She was not to be left alone, even then. Mrs. Hodges needed counsel, on the meals for the end of the week: there was not enough pork for Sunday if the whole party were to be present, for Mr. Knightley had sent his best loin to Miss Bates. Should Madam prefer duck?— William Larkins had reported there were farmyard fowl fattening up.

When the good cook had gone, came some minutes for reflection – but Emma did not wish to think of theft; of ungrateful women; or of deception practised on her and its outcome in the courts of Surrey. She hoped the two female miscreants would not go to prison.— No! She still could not bear to imagine the Baroness shut up, her fine gowns gone threadbare in the cells at Dorking.— She prayed for clemency on the part of the magistrate, and wondered, even, if John Knightley might intercede for her.

But she must not interfere again. Happiness – indeed, perfect happiness – must come from understanding where she had thought she too perfectly understood, that there were complications, matters kept hidden that were not intended to be revealed. She did not wish to know the real facts surrounding the Baroness – she would ask Mr. Knightley if he could save her. Yet the Abdy woman might bring her down.— Emma, putting her hands to her ears, found her joy fading with the unexpected speed with which it had come.

Nothing, as Emma was doomed to see, whether she would hold on to her precious new-found contentment or not, had been as it seemed. All along, she had been mistaken— mistaken, to beg her husband to grant permission for the Abdy barn, to a felon, perhaps a stranger to her own family for many long years; in all likelihood not even recognised by the honest ostler or his father, when she had come with three bastard children to cajole money from them, at Highbury.

She had been mistaken, again, when she had believed the tale spun by a liar and thief who posed as a French noblewoman, but who was in equal probability as much a denizen of the slums of Bristol as was young Abdy's sister – both women whores and vagrants – kept by slavers, beaten by their masters as they went out to vend their souls.— Here Emma shivered so violently, that she was drawn to rise, and go over to the fire. The sunlight and fine furniture of Donwell Abbey had never seemed so greatly welcome to her, as they did now.

Then there was the matchmaking.— Emma, whose spirits were irrepressible, and whose faults were not one-tenth as numerous as her perfections (in the eyes of those, like Mr. Knightley and Mrs. Weston, who loved her, at any rate) found her heart lift and her good humour recover, when she recalled the occasion, deep in the midst of her first night of happiness with Mr. Knightley, of her breathless promise to him that she would meddle no longer in the lives and loves of others. She had had – Emma would always have, however great her abandon into ecstasy – the sense of being in the right – the desire to inform Mr. Knightley that he, also, had attempted to make a match, for his brother; but she had not had the opportunity to hear Mr. Knightley's reply, for he had kissed her, just then, too hard.

It had been something to the effect that news would arrive soon, on that score. She had responded to his caresses and had not thought more of it; a flush of reminiscence coupled with a mischievous smile succeeded each other, as Emma walked this time to the windows of the dining-room and opened them on to a lawn green and gold with the first rays of an autumnal sun. Whatever George – at last she had called his name! – whatever the dear man had planned for his brother, it could no longer be marriage with the woman who had styled herself Baroness. Emma began to see the humour in the situation; and as a figure walked quietly up the lawn and paused by the window, she was no longer able to resist indulging her desire to laugh.

"Mrs. Knightley?" Jane Fairfax stood by the dining-room windows of Donwell Abbey; she was pale, but Emma saw she wore a fine comb studded with precious stones, set in her dark hair. Her expression was serious: Emma swallowed her laughter as best she could.

"My dear Miss Fairfax! Come in." It was a pleasure, to Emma, to show the poor governess that others such as Mrs. Elton or Mrs. Smallridge, might call her Jane, and ask of her a thousand menial tasks.— Here at Donwell she would remain as she had always been, Miss Fairfax, esteemed niece of Highbury's best-loved spinster, dear Miss Bates.

"I have news to bring you which you may not find pleasant," said the young woman, in a quiet and measured tone. "I will be frank – I do not know how to commence, Mrs. Knightley. But I must inform you – I am engaged to be married! You must be the first to know."

Emma's mind went through imaginings impossible to record, so fast-moving and untoward were they.— For Jane could surely not have decided to marry Captain Brocklehurst, rouge and white gown and fine slippers and all? No, it could not be! Had Mrs. Churchill died, then? Had Frank been called to Enscombe, as he had been summoned by his aunt all of four years ago, because she was departing this world? And if this were so, surely it would be in the worst of taste, that he should propose marriage to Miss Fairfax, while his wife lay dying? But Frank was not known for his good taste, Emma reflected; had she not incurred Jane's dislike herself by joining him in a flirtation which was most unsavoury for all who witnessed it?— But was Frank not, perhaps, another such as his brother-in-law? Why did he bring the Captain to Highbury alone, if not to indulge in a friendship which must not be spoken of? Did Frank too, with all his posies and his fine words, love the Captain more than he loved Jane?

One other possibility remained, when Emma had banished all these from her mind. It was too far-fetched. She knew of lonely women who had joined the movement for the Second Coming of the Messiah, who had worshipped Joanna Southcott and her famous box, at Exeter. Did Jane mean to wed the Lord? Was she betrothed to Christ?

An image of the Baroness and Jane together succeeded this; then Emma, staring still at her unexpected visitor, began to see the comb in Miss Fairfax's dark hair.— Yes, she said to herself, and with an effort restrained a cry of surprise. It is old Mrs. Knightley's jewellery that Jane Fairfax wears! She cannot have been presented them by Mr. Knightley – not by George . . .

"I am engaged to John Knightley," said Jane Fairfax in a voice that was still modest and low. "We met at Cromer; we had both lost our loves – John his Isabella, if you will pardon me, Emma – and I Frank Churchill, to whom I had been betrothed. In speaking of our sadness, we found comfort; and we shall find love. I shall be your sister, dear Emma. We have at times not been as one, despite knowing each other all our lives."

With these words Jane Fairfax began to weep. Emma, who saw she must put her best face on it – and who was able, within a very short time, to convince herself that she alone was responsible for the match – went forward to comfort her; and it was thus, clasped as sisters should be, that Mr. Knightley – who appeared very pleased with himself indeed – found his Emma and the future Mrs. John Knightley in the dining-room at Donwell.

"My breakfast does not come, Emma," said Mr. Knightley; and Emma, seeing he teased her, instructed him to pull the bell-rope if he wished to be served.

"This is splendid news, Emma," said Mr. Knightley, after Jane Fairfax had been persuaded to accept tea – but no more. "I was informed, when John returned from Norfolk.— I kept the matter quiet, as our mother's estates had to be settled, to the benefit of the new couple – and I teased you on the subject of the Baroness, my dear Emma: forgive me!"

Emma smiled; though she resolved to pay Mr. Knightley out for his deception, when she next had the chance.

"We shall have the wedding here in October," continued Mr. Knightley. "And you, my dear Emma, are the one to make our nephews and nieces happy at the arrival of a new mother – is she not, dear Miss Fairfax?"

Jane Fairfax was too overcome to do anything other than sip at her tea and murmur her willing assent.

26

$\mathcal{T}$ ime passed. A few more tomorrows and the boating party would have come and gone; the new lake, dredged and cleaned for the purpose, much admired; and the engagement of John Knightley, its proud owner, to the secretive Miss Fairfax, be known by all and very thoroughly discussed.

What could not be known, in advance, was the number of guests Mrs. Knightley – for it was she, as the future Mrs. John Knightley declared herself too shy to issue any invitations – was determined to summon to the event. Mrs. Elton – just returned from Lyme with Mrs. Smallridge, and Miss Whynne in attendance on all the children, for Emma's nephews and nieces had been happy to be informed that another trip to the seaside lay in store – was unable to direct the exclusive nature of the boating party, or to prevent the whole of Highbury being cordially welcomed to the site of the new lake. Had she known, she would very likely have sent a refusal before it was too late. That Mrs. Cole and Mrs. Gilbert were expected – and that old Abdy was to be conveyed there in a chair, for his last glimpse of a stretch of water he had navigated as a lad, would have been reprehensible to the Vicar's wife; and Mr. Elton, as it occurred on the evening of the festivities, was sent to Mr. Perry for medicaments to counter the shock and sadness of his Augusta;— but, unfortunately for any of the few who did not attend, Mr. Perry along with Mrs. Perry and all the little Perrys, was also on the shores of the very fine lake that day, and those who felt unwell must go unvisited.

Emma took particular care to demonstrate her new sense of a wholeness in the village, on the occasion of the boating party. She accepted invitations from those who were newly arrived in Highbury, and even from those who were in trade – and she reminded John Knightley, when he remonstrated with her, that the very best people, such as Mr. Weston, made their living in this fashion; and that Miss Bates, who had not a scruple when it came to entertaining the Westons, should be listened to more often; for her words were inclined to spell out the truth a great deal more than the pontifications of certain distinguished lawyers and members of other elevated professions.

She did not say that Miss Bates's odd habits with speech had led to an understanding of the predilections of those she spoke of – though Emma thought she could recall very well that Miss Bates, on the occasion of Emma's visit to her apartment in the main street of Highbury, had looked from the window and muttered "bugger Brocklehurst"— though Emma could not swear to it.

It was seen by all, on the very fine day which was selected for the boating party, that John Knightley's prophecies of stormy weather were quite unfounded. His brother's excellent good humour, as calm and un-ruffled as the day, was also remarked upon; and when, late in the afternoon, the already large throng on the cobbled shore was joined by a party of wild-looking young people, no one saw him complain, or his happy mien falter in the least.

There was too much to talk of: that John Knightley and Jane would live at Hartfield and the school would be permanently established there, was one weighty topic; as was Mrs. Smallridge's search for a governess, and the strangeness of her having asked Miss Bates if she would like to take the position. Emma had had to quash the suggestion rapidly. Besides which, there was talk still of the thieving – it remained a rumour, for Mr. Knightley had brought no charges, and Mrs. Elton believed her friend's ring to have been retrieved from the piano at Lyme and somehow whisked up to her at Highbury by reason of its being the property of so magical a person as Lady Carinthia Bragge. The maid at Donwell Abbey said nothing, but there had been talk. The happiness which reigned there made any suggestion of loss or theft quite ridiculous.

There was, however, a talking point which, arising as it did on the day of the boating party, was almost unstoppable in its gaining of detail and credence as it passed from simple village family to those who should have known better than to permit its progress amongst the crowd.

A young woman, very beautiful, with dark ringlets and very strong dark eyebrows, had been seen to step into a small rowing-boat and set out across the lake, towards a small wooded island in the centre.

Some said the young lady had kissed Mrs. Weston, who had spoken and laughed very tearfully; and that they had been joined by Mr. Knightley himself, who had wandered off with them to a distant glade. It was reported, by Mrs. Smallridge, that the young stranger had borne more than a passing resemblance to the charming baroness, who had come to Highbury with dear Jane: she even expressed her desire that this young lady might consider the post of governess to her daughters.

It was possible that a cousin, a niece – some said more – had come into the Knightley family. A rumour, short-lived by reason of the esteem in which both the squire of Donwell Abbey and the good lady who once had been the governess to Emma were held, had the dark stranger as their daughter; and it had "poor Miss Taylor" at Hartfield all those years out of a desire to be near Mr. Knightley. The child, put to boarding-school at Bristol, had gone to the bad; she had fallen in with young Abdy's sister when the latter was taken on as a maid at the Sucklings' mansion near there. A large quantity of jewels had subsequently disappeared. No one knew for certain. What was certain was that Emma Knightley stepped into the rowing-boat with her friend, and they set off together for the island – where they remained until it was almost dark. As John Knightley was heard to remark, the equinoctial storms were due to descend on Surrey at any time now; and he would only feel safe when his sister-in-law and her companion had rowed home across still waters already rippling with the first winds of the autumnal gales to come. His betrothed, Miss Fairfax, had, as ever, no comment to make at all.